Now! Read the Compelling Adventure
Based on Warner Bros. TV Series

KUNG FU

Follow the dramatic odyssey
of the singular figure you
know as CAINE.

How will this half-Chinese
half-American Shaolin monk
respond to the injustice of
a "frame" and forced labor?

How can Caine use his unique
training to withstand the
inhuman punishment meted out
by the silver mine owners?

How can Caine's philosophy
overcome the hold of superstition upon those who fear it?

Published By
WARNER PAPERBACK LIBRARY

KUNG FU

#3

Superstition

A novel by
Howard Lee

Based on the television story by David Moessinger
from the Warner Bros. Television hit series created by
Ed Spielman and starring David Carradine on ABC.

WARNER
PAPERBACK
LIBRARY

A Warner Communications Company

WARNER PAPERBACK LIBRARY EDITION
First Printing: December, 1973
Second Printing: June, 1974

Cover illustration by Jim Sharpe

Warner Paperback Library is a division of Warner Books, Inc.,
75 Rockefeller Plaza, New York, N.Y. 10019.

A Warner Communications Company

Printed in the United States of America

SUPERSTITION

ONE

The wind was carrying parts of the town away.

It ripped a chunk of jigsaw trim off the roof of the abandoned hotel and sent it spinning through the rain to splash into a wide, deep puddle in the center of the main street.

From the wall of the boarded-up general store the wet wind tore posters announcing events that had happened last year and the year before.

A piece of the gilded balcony railing, brought in originally all the way from San Francisco, was creaking and flapping. Finally it made a rasping, shrieking sound and was blown free of the Silver Creek Opera House.

Caine came walking into the town from the north

end—a long, lanky young man, barefooted, wearing a pair of faded trousers and a weathered jacket. A bedroll was slung over his shoulder. He carried no guns, no weapon of any kind. The rain beat down on him, washing away the last of the dust of a long, dry journey on foot.

The Opera House creaked again, and a gilded wooden ball popped off its roof and fell into a muddy alley. Two black mutt dogs barked at Caine, but didn't come out from under the swayback wooden porch that sheltered them. Rain water came gushing down through a rusty drain, spurting out in mid-air where the tin sluice pipe had cracked.

From up ahead came wheezing harmonica music. A narrow building with the words "Estling's Food Drink" whitewashed on its one small window seemed to be still in business.

Caine stepped up onto the plank sidewalk and into the thin saloon.

Sitting by himself at one of the three bare tables was a young cowboy. He had his booted feet up on the table and was playing the harmonica.

Estling, a fat man with a doughy face, was behind the small bar, leaning on it while he played a game of cooncan with a one-eyed customer. He frowned in Caine's direction.

Caine, halting on the muddy wood floor just inside the doorless doorway, said, "I would like to buy some food." A trickle of rain ran along the brim of his hat and onto the floor.

"You don't have to go slopping all over the place, messing everything up," Estling said.

The one-eyed man was old. A week's growth of

white stubble bristled on his leathery face. He glanced over at Caine, squinting his only eye at him for a second, then turned his attention back to the grimy playing cards before him on the bar top.

"I am sorry." Caine moved closer to the dough-faced saloon-keeper. "I would like to purchase some beans and salt."

The cowboy took the harmonica away from his lips and wiped the saliva from it on the leg of his woolly chaps. "He talks real nice for a Chink," he observed.

Estling concentrated on his card game for the next minute. Then, poking a thick thumb in the direction of the single shelf behind him, he said, "Whisky or brandy. You can take your pick."

"I need only food."

A ripple moved down Estling's chest and stomach as he shrugged. "I already told you what we got to offer. Whisky or brandy is it."

"He must think this is the old days," said the cowboy, "when all the mines was working."

Caine turned away from the bar and walked out of the place.

The wind was still at work, ripping away shingles and ragged strips of roofing paper from the dozens of closed-up buildings that made up Silver Creek.

He walked on through the morning rain. In the next block he saw a supply store, a mean, low building of gray wood. It looked to be open.

A huge orange cat lolled on the counter, paying no attention to the two dusty gray mice who were chewing their way into a sack of meal on the floor in the corner.

9

There was no one in the shadowy room. A tarnished call-bell sat on the counter between the cat and a round molding cheese. Caine slapped the bell twice.

The obese cat moved its head slightly in his direction, but there was no other response.

On the floor before the counter was a bushel basket filled with dry beans. A paper sign stuck in among the beans offered: Beans/2¢ A Pound.

After giving the bell one more ring, Caine reached into his haversack, found two pennies, and put them on the counter. Picking up a handful of beans, he dropped them into a scale hanging above the counter. He was adding a second handful when a boot hit the wood floor behind him.

"Hold it right there, Chinaman."

Caine dropped the beans into the scale, then turned to face Estling. "Do you also own this store?"

"Never you mind what I own and what I don't own." Estling held a Springfield rifle pointed at him. On the doughy man's shirt front a tarnished star was pinned. "You're under arrest."

"I was only measuring a pound of beans," Caine told him. "For which I left payment."

"Save your story for your trial, Chinaman." Estling ordered Caine out into the rainy street.

TWO

The young cowboy was sitting up straight, feet on the warped floor of the little saloon. The tip of his harmonica protruded from the pocket of his checked shirt. He was whistling, his tongue pressed up against the back of his teeth.

The one-eyed man was seated at another table, his knobby hands folded around a nearly empty glass of brandy.

Estling cleared his throat as a tall, wide-shouldered man came striding in out of the rain.

The big man stepped behind the bar and brushed aside the grimy deck of cards. He reached down and came up with a claw hammer in his hand. "Court is now in session," he announced as he hit the bar top several times. "What's the prisoner's name?"

Prodding Caine with the barrel of the Springfield rifle, Estling said, "Tell Mr. Banner your name."

"I am called Caine."

"That's all your name?" asked Banner.

"Kwai Chang Caine."

"You're a Chinaman, huh?"

"I was born in China."

"What you doing in these parts, Caine?"

"I am but passing through."

The cowboy halted his whistling to laugh. "That's what most everybody does nowadays."

"Let me remind you, MacTell," said Banner, "there is a trial going on."

"I know that. Don't I watch every dang trial you have?" MacTell returned to his whistling.

"Now, Caine," continued Banner, "I understand there's some pretty serious charges been brought against you by the sheriff here."

Estling cleared his throat again, spit in the direction of the tin-can cuspidor, and said, "That's certainly so, Judge. I caught this Chinaman redhanded stealing food and supplies out of the Silver Creek Emporium."

"What you got to say to that, Caine?"

"I left payment there."

"Yeah? How about that, Estling?"

The fat man shrugged. "Would I arrest a paying customer? He was helping himself to everything that wasn't nailed down."

Rubbing the tip of the hammer handle over his chin, Banner said, "Any other witnesses?"

"Only me," said Estling. "And I saw him plain."

"Well now, Caine, you been charged with stealing," said Banner. "Got anything to say?"

"I am not guilty."

The wide-shouldered man hit the bar top a few times more. "The court has reached a decision," he said. "We hereby declare the prisoner guilty as charged."

"Now ain't that a surprise," said the young cowboy.

Banner went on. "By the mercy of the court the prisoner is offered a choice of sentences. Six months' labor up at the Lucky Susan Mine . . . or two years in jail. What's it going to be?"

Caine said, "To choose one or the other would be to concur in a falsehood."

"Since the accused has no preference," said Banner, "the court must decide for him. Caine, you are hereby sentenced to six months' labor at the Lucky Susan mine."

The big man came around to the front of the bar. He had drawn his six-shooter from his holster. "We're going to take us a little trip up into the hills now, Caine. You try to get away, try anything tricky at all, and it'll be my duty to shoot you dead. You understand?"

Caine looked at him levelly. There was no need to reply.

"Might be almost better to get shot," said MacTell, swinging his boots back atop his table. "Better than having them dead Indians . . ."

"Shut up, MacTell," warned Banner. "Or maybe

13

you'll find yourself working a spell up at the mine, too."

"Not me," said the cowboy. "I'm a completely honest man."

Estling and the cowboy watched, their guns ready, as Banner fitted Caine's wrists into the manacles bolted to the floor of his wagon. Caine obeyed the brusque orders impassively, his eyes on a leaf determinedly resisting the wind's efforts to dislodge it from its branch. He assessed the possibility of escape: no. The risk was too great.

The chance had been earlier, before the mock trial. But then he hadn't been sure—he'd told himself that the court would clarify matters, and he'd be free to continue on his way, preferably (but not necessarily) with the beans in his pouch. Not that his way had been so clear . . .

The wind-whipped leaf held his attention, stirring a memory from boyhood. He thought of himself, a solemn-eyed child, newly admitted into the Shaolin temple.

He was sweeping the courtyard free of leaves when he stopped to stare at a leaf, nearly the last on the tree, and found himself silently willing the leaf to endure, to remain.

"What troubles you, grasshopper?" The voice, warm and concerned, was that of the blind master, Po, whose silent approach had escaped the boy's notice.

A little alarmed at being caught idle, he had answered timidly, "It seems sad, master. The leaf is hanging on bravely, but the wind will conquer soon. And the leaf's struggle will have been useless."

"And do you think that a man's life may be like that?" Po questioned gently. "That a boy—for instance—may see his parents, and his grandparents, swept away like leaves before the wind, while he clings lonely to a branch, fighting to remain, but knowing he too must fall in his turn?"

"Something of that I—I had thought about," Kwai Chang Caine had said, a knot of grief tightening his throat.

"Sit down, grasshopper. Let us talk a bit longer about leaves, since you have much business with them."

Though he sat at a respectful distance from the master, the boy felt oddly as if Po had wrapped a fatherly arm around him.

"When the leaf falls, does it disappear?" Po continued.

"No, master." The boy smiled ruefully. "Or else I shouldn't have to spend my days sweeping them."

"And when you have swept them up, what then?"

"I carry them to the garden," Caine replied. "They go around the roots of young plants, to protect them from the cold of winter, or they cover the vegetable beds. Next spring they'll make the earth more fruitful."

"So, grasshopper. If they are then so useful off the tree, is the wind doing wrong when it blows them off?"

Caine hesitated. "No, master, but . . ."

"What seems to you a battle is not. The wind is a necessary force of change, enabling the leaf to ful-

fill its destiny. It is not the conqueror, nor is the leaf conquered."

The boy was silent for a moment. Finally, diffidently, he asked, "May not the leaf that remains yet fear the prospect of falling?"

Po smiled warmly. "Perhaps. Or perhaps it welcomes its destiny. All sorts of winds blow throughout any life, and without the changes they bring, there would be no life. But you may put aside your broom and your leaves now, grasshopper, for I think it is suppertime."

Manacled to the wagon, Caine thought: this is a changing wind, and whether it brings a new winter or a new spring I cannot yet know. But his face had a smile totally without irony as he turned to Banner and said, "I was seeking a relative, Daniel Caine. Do you know of him?"

Banner paused, shaken by the expression on his captive's face. "He's either a fool—or a saint," he told himself. Aloud he said, "Naw. Never heard of him."

The trail cut up through gray rock, the incline growing steeper and steeper as the open wagon climbed higher.

Banner in a yellow slicker and black Stetson held the reins of the two horses.

The wind came zigzagging down the trail, splashing rain against the wagon, flinging scraps of brush, scattering dirt and pebbles.

"Used to be a lot of mines going around here," Banner said, looking back over his shoulder.

16

Caine did not reply. He sat quietly, the rain beating down on him.

"Not any more, though," said Banner. "That's why Silver Creek is like it is. When the rest of the mines played out, that was the death of the town."

The horses strained, snorting, working their way up the incline.

"Now the Lucky Susan Mine's the only one going," said the big man after a while.

Finally, after another half-hour of rough climbing, the trail leveled out on a sort of broad plateau. Up ahead rose a high timber fence.

"This is it."

Nailed to the left of the gate was a sign—*Lucky Susan Mine, Property Of Jonathan Sterne Mining Co. TRESPASSERS WILL BE SHOT.*

"Forget about what MacTell was sounding off about down there," said Banner. "About dead Indians and all. You'll do a lot better if you just forget about that, Caine."

THREE

All Boetticher's clothes were a mourning black.
His trousers, his high-top boots, his shirt, necker-
chief, and leather vest, his wide-brim sombrero, his
holster, and the bone-handled Colt .44 it carried. He
was standing now at the peak of a hilly San Francisco street. It was the first hour after sunset, and
a thick gray fog was rolling up off the Bay far below
to the right. Away downhill the clopping of horses
pulling a trolley by sounded.

Boetticher was a lean, tall man. He was only a
year over thirty, but he had the face, especially the
eyes, of a man ten years older. A weather-beaten,
unsmiling face. In his right hand was a slip of ruled
paper with an address scrawled on it. Boetticher had
obtained the address a week ago from a man in

Denver. To get it, only a few words and some numbers, he'd had to work on the man half the day.

"There was a time," he thought to himself, "when I couldn't have . . ." He allowed the thought to fade away. "That was a long time ago."

Stuffing the piece of paper back into his shirt pocket, Boetticher began walking.

They were starting to build a good many houses in this part of San Francisco now. Not as fancy as the places the railroad barons and the silver kings and the other millionaires had built for themselves on Nob Hill, but big, substantial homes, nonetheless. Two and three stories, wooden, with protruding bay windows and much carved gingerbread ornamentation.

A few blocks farther on, the city ended. Then there was only sand, square miles of nothing but sandhills between here and the Pacific.

Boetticher located the house he was seeking in the next block. A tall new place, freshly painted a pale green. The fog was settling in all around, blurring its edges, hiding the dozens of shutters, cutting off the tips of spires and cupolas. Out on the Bay, foghorns were calling.

The lean, black-clad man circled the home, watching the windows. Light showed at two places on the lower floor, not at all on the second floor. One light was at the rear of the house in what was probably the kitchen, another closer to the front.

Boetticher chose this nearer window. He scaled the wrought-iron fence and worked his way through the shrubs and across the new lawn.

Grabbing hold of the window sill, he boosted himself up. The lighted room beyond was a study. And there at the desk was the man he wanted, the man who was now calling himself Lofton.

Boetticher drew his pistol. Using it as a hammer, he swung up, smashing the glass out of the window with three sharp blows.

"Good Lord!" exclaimed Lofton, jumping up from behind the desk.

Boetticher climbed carefully over the sill, keeping the .44 aimed at the other man.

From off in the kitchen came a scream. "Oh, Mr. Lofton! What is it, what is it?"

"Tell her it's nothing to worry about," said Boetticher.

"Who . . . ?"

"Tell her!"

"Nothing to worry about, Eloise," Lofton called out. "I simply had a little accident."

Walking by him, Boetticher shoved the study door shut. "Good to see you again," he said. "You haven't aged well."

Lofton was short and heavy, in his middle forties, pink-faced, wearing a silk smoking jacket. "Who . . . I don't know you."

"My name is Boetticher."

Lofton exhaled all the breath he had in him. He sat back down in his desk chair. "The kid brother," he said after a while.

"I couldn't be *Dan* Boetticher, could I?" Boetticher said. "Because we both know he's dead and buried, don't we?"

"Yes, I . . ."

"At least, you know he's dead. You, the three of you, didn't wait around to bury Dan, way I hear."

"Listen, it wasn't me who . . ."

"Wasn't you who killed my brother for the cash he'd made from selling out his cattle ranch? Wasn't you who stole his wife afterwards?"

"You don't understand," began Lofton.

"Oh, I understand. I understand that with your share of the money you came here to Frisco and started yourself a nice little banking business. Been prospering, haven't you, Mr. Lofton?"

"I can," offered Lofton, "give you back the money. My piece of it, that is. I never really wanted to take it, but the other fellows, those other two . . ."

"Yeah, that's a fine idea. Give me the money."

"You have to come down to my bank with me in the morn—"

Boetticher's laugh was dry and humorless. "You better have that money right here in this cosy little room of yours."

"Well, yes." Lofton pushed himself back from the desk. "I do keep some emergency cash around." He reached out toward a drawer in his desk.

"If your hand comes out with anything but money in it, Mr. Lofton, you'll be awfully soon dead."

Lofton pulled the drawer gradually open and lifted out a tin box. "The money's in here."

"Open it right up, then hand me ten thousand dollars."

"Ten thousand dollars? Why, my share was only . . ."

"You know how things get garbled, Mr. Lofton," said Boetticher. "I was over in Australia, working in

21

the gold fields, when you boys were doing all this. But the figure I heard Dan had was thirty thousand dollars. Isn't that what it was?"

"Well, yes, yes, it was thirty thousand," admitted Lofton. "What I'm trying to explain to you is this. I wasn't a full, an equal, partner. It was the other two, Avison and Gunther, who got the biggest shares. I only got five thousand for myself."

"Oh, that's too bad, Mr. Lofton, because you're still going to have to pay me ten. Call the rest interest," said Boetticher. "I'm going to need that money for my work."

"Work?" Lofton pulled the black money box open with unsteady hands.

"I been back from Australia six months," he explained. "When I got home, I found out about what had happened to Dan and Marianne. Know what I been doing ever since?"

Lofton shook his head several times. "No, no, I don't."

"Why, I been looking for you, looking for the three of you," said Boetticher. "And you're the first one I run down."

"Listen, Boetticher . . . I never wanted no part of what those others done. Lord, man, it was five years ago and . . ."

"You was just a mere boy of forty," cut in Boetticher. "Young and impressionable, easy led astray." He stuck his free hand into the cash, grabbing up a fistful.

"I never had a thing to do with killing your brother," insisted Lofton. "With the actual killing, you know."

22

"You merely stood around and watched," said Boetticher. "Watched while them other two boys shot him four times in the chest and twice in the head. Later, when they raped his wife, you probably only watched that, too."

"Nobody raped her."

"You took her along with you simply to have somebody to talk to, maybe?"

"You don't understand how it was."

"Nope, I wasn't there." After he thrust the big bills in his pocket, Boetticher moved the barrel of the .44 closer to the seated man's head. "Where's Marianne now? Did they kill her when they was finished?"

"No," said Lofton. "I don't know. Maybe Gunther would know. You got to realize that I parted company with them soon as I took my five thousand share. Said goodbye and headed right for San Francisco here."

"Guess I better have me a talk with Gunther, then. Where is he?"

His eyes on the gun, Lofton shook his head. "I don't know. I never heard about him from that day to this."

Boetticher pushed the gun closer. "Where is he?"

"I swear I don't know. I swear!" said Lofton. "That was part of our deal. Separate, change our names, have nothing to do with each other from there on out."

"What about Avison?"

"Same goes for him. I never . . ."

The pistol barrel touched the pink-faced man's cheek. "Fellow I happened to run into in Denver thought different. He had the notion you see Avison once in a while," said Boetticher. "Unless you want this gun to go off right now, Mr. Lofton, you better tell me where Avison is now and what name he goes by."

"All right, all right." Lofton pulled his head back so the gun wasn't touching him. Slowly, after licking his lips, he told Boetticher where Avison was, what name he was living under.

"Thank you very much, Mr. Lofton."

"Now . . . are you going to leave me be?"

"No, you bushwhacker, I'm going to kill you." Boetticher fired four shots into him.

FOUR

A low house stood some distance from the other mine buildings, alone behind a disorderly picket fence. When the door of the house opened, a slender, dark-haired woman showed briefly, dressed in gingham, in the small parlor. A chunky blond man, in a tight-fitting slicker, came slogging through the rain from the isolated house to the office building.

Caine, who stood silently beside a window of the office, watched the approaching man.

Banner was sitting in the desk chair, his back to the cluttered rolltop. He finished constructing a cigarette for himself, licked the seam, and put it between his lips. "That'll be Sterne trotting over from his little love nest," he said.

The door rattled, then opened. "Good, good," said Sterne, his small eyes fixed on Caine. He had a high-pitched fluty voice. "I was starting to think maybe the well'd run dry." He began to shake out of his coat.

"Always more recruits to be had." Banner swung around and plucked a wooden match out of the tin cup on the desk. After lighting his cigarette, he asked, "How's Lucky Susan getting along?"

"Come on over to the workbench and I'll show you."

"I was referring to your dear wife." Banner eased up out of the chair.

Frowning, Sterne said, "She's fine, just fine."

"Always glad to hear that, Johnny," said Banner. "Down there in Silver Creek, with all the advantages and pleasures of city life, I get to worrying about Lucky Susan up here all by herself."

"Her name is Susan," said Sterne. "You don't have to stick Lucky in front of it every damn time you mention her."

"Guess I can't help thinking of her as the source of our luck. All the other mines have played out, while we're still going strong."

The blond chunky Sterne hung his rain gear on a claw-footed hatrack near his desk. He then walked over to Caine. "What'd you bring us this time, Banner, a Chinaman?"

"I guess he is. Don't matter much one way or the other." Banner crossed to the workbench. "Estling caught him stealing provisions out of the Emporium. We give him a fair trial. It was the decision of the court that he spend six months or so working in the silver mine."

Sterne asked, "What's your name?"

"I am Caine."

"Hey, now." Banner was bending over some lumps of blue-black ore that sat beside a balance scale atop the bench. "This stuff looks better than what we been getting lately."

"Yeah, we hit a new vein while you were down enjoying yourself in Silver Creek." Sterne joined the other man at the work table. "My preliminary tests indicate the ratio of silver to lead in this stuff is near double what we've been getting."

Banner laughed. "Seems like our luck is holding," he said. "All our lien holders will be happy to hear this."

"I can still use a few more men," said Sterne, turning to study Caine. "You used to doing hard work where you come from, Chinaman?"

Caine returned his gaze steadily. This was a question that required no answer.

"You look like you got the idea you was railroaded or something," said Sterne. "Well, Caine, let me give you a little friendly advice before I assign you to your crew. We got a really effective way of improving the men who come here to the Lucky Susan Mine to work for us. We can change thieves, like you, and murderers, robbers, bums, and brawlers. Our system works with all kinds."

"Take a look out of this window here," suggested Banner, beckoning.

Caine stepped to the indicated window.

"We got it set up over there, so it'll be out of the sight of the house," said Banner. "Don't want it to upset Luck— Mrs. Sterne none. We never got around to naming it, but the men call it the Box."

Out there in the rainy afternoon was a shack, a squat building with walls and roof of metal.

Sterne, behind Caine, explained, "It's all iron. So it can take heat or cold and increase them real good. When the sun's hot, that box is sizzling as an oven inside. But come nighttime, it's freezing. You've chosen to arrive on an unusual day, Caine. Usually it's real hot up here in the daytime. Meaning anybody going into the Box is sure of a nice baking."

"That Box does more good than all the lectures and whuppings in the world," said Banner.

" 'Course," added Sterne, "you may never have to spend a day or two in the Box, Caine. If you cooperate with us right from the start."

"What," Caine asked slowly, "is *cooperate?*"

"It's real simple," answered Sterne. "All you got to remember is our two golden rules. First off, keep working hard every minute of your shift. Second, stay out of trouble." He opened the office door and called out, "Hey, Nolan!"

"You'll also," said Banner, "get a reward for cooperating with us."

"That's right," picked up the mine-owner. "You'll earn yourself a credit of ten cents for each day of good behavior."

"Think about that, now, Caine. By the time you end your little stay with us you'll maybe have eighteen bucks in your poke," said Banner, chuckling. "That'll make you pretty well off for a China-man, won't it, now?"

A freckled man in a black slicker showed in the doorway. He carried a shotgun under his arm. "Called me?"

"New man for you," said Sterne. "Name of Caine. Put him in with Rupp's gang."

"Okay, coolie," said Nolan. "Let's get it moving."

When Caine was in the doorway, Banner called out, "Caine!"

He turned, waiting.

"Don't forget what we told you about cooperat-ing." Banner laughed once more.

FIVE

The iron door of the Box made a harsh, rasping sound when it was pulled open. The bearded guard who'd tugged it open bent and squinted into the metal-walled shack. "You can come on out of there now, Frisco," he said. "Unless you like it too much to leave." He reached inside.

Caine's escort had stopped to watch. "Guess they 'splained to you about the Box," he said.

Caine inclined his head slightly: yes.

"Keep it in mind."

The bearded guard grunted as he pulled a thin, hollow-eyed man out of the punishment shack. "We got somebody else anxious to get in there, Frisco. You got to leave it."

The thin Frisco, held upright by the guard, blinked at the heavy rain and the gray afternoon without seeming to really see anything. When the guard let go, the man swayed, took a step clear of the Box, and fell straight forward into the mud.

Wiping an oily brown splash from his trousers, the bearded guard said, "I got to remember not to wear my good clothes."

Two other guards came across the plateau with a struggling heavyset man between them.

The bearded guard grabbed up Frisco by the shirt collar and dragged him off through the mud.

"No, please!" protested the man whose turn it was next. "You ain't goin' to put me in there."

A fist across the back of the neck quieted him and he was heaved into the Box.

Nolan, Caine's guard, said, "Be thankful that ain't you."

Caine, feeling the suffering of the first prisoner and the panic of the second, asked, "How do you know it is not?"

The freckled guard gave a quick, puzzled shrug before saying, "Let's us get along."

There were four barracks buildings. They stood side by side, long low buildings painted a forlorn brown. Two raw outhouse toilets were located to the rear of the barracks.

Frisco, half walking and half crawling, was tossed into the first barracks building.

Looking in at the open door as he passed, Caine noticed that none of the man's fellow workers went immediately near him.

Nolan stopped in front of the next building, fished

a key out of his pocket with the hand that wasn't clutching the shotgun. "Here's your new lodgings," he announced as the door opened.

Caine, with no hesitation, walked into the murky room. Once he was inside, the door was shut and locked.

Nine men were in there. A row of wooden bunks ran down each side of the room. On the bunk nearest him a man was already stretched out on his back, a hand over his face, snoring. Three wooden buckets of water sat on the dirt floor at the back of the room. Most of the other men were circling these, washing off the dirt of a day in the mine. The only light came from two tallow candles stuck in tin cans that were nailed to two of the support beams. There were thick iron bars on all five of the small windows.

A tall man with bright yellow hair was very slowly and deliberately wiping his hands, one finger at a time, on a dirty towel. He came closer to Caine, his head cocked to the right. "Well sir, a Chinaman," he said. "Maybe that'll change our luck."

One of the other men laughed.

The first man asked, "Boy, where'd they find you?"

Caine's silence nettled him. More roughly, he demanded, "What's the matter? No speakee?"

"I am Caine."

"Now ain't that something," he said jeeringly. "He's got a name!" His glance demanded the admiration of his listeners. Turning back to Caine, he said warningly, "So do I, boy. Mine's Rupp. And what I say goes around here. Got that?"

For a moment Caine's failure to answer annoyed Rupp, then he laughed. Silence means consent, doesn't it? "You keep that in mind and we'll make out real fine, you and me." He strode back to the wash buckets. "Tomorrow we'll see how you work. Denver, show it where to bed down."

The man called Denver had been sitting on the edge of his bunk. He was big, broad-chested, in his fifties. His face was lined and weathered by years spent outdoors and not in mines. He rose off the bunk, smiling at Caine. "We only got one empty, Caine," he said. "So you don't get much choice. That one down on the end there." He walked along to the bed as he spoke.

There was only a thin, tattered blanket on the wooden frame of the bed.

"Not much, but it's a shade better than sleeping directly on the dirt," said Denver.

Caine bowed slightly, acknowledging the man's rough courtesy. He unslung his bedroll and set it on his new bunk.

A medium-sized young man with shaggy dark hair drifted over. "Good thing you got your own blanket. You'll need it. Gets colder than a witch's backside up here nighttimes."

Caine's eyes moved to the barred window. He was looking out at the dusk.

Denver watched him for a moment. "I imagine I know what you're thinking, Caine," he said. "I thought about it, too, quite a lot, the first weeks I was here." He let out a sigh, shaking his head. "Two weeks back, four of the boys from the next barracks tried to sneak out of here in the night. *You* tell him what happened, Gil."

"They didn't make it," said the dark-haired young man.

"They sure didn't," said Denver. "Banner's boys caught them in no time. Banner . . . lined them up in front of us and shot the four of them."

Gil's face grew taut, remembering.

"So what you got to face up to," Denver told Caine, "is there's no way out of this here camp."

Caine said, "When a man has served his time . . . is there a way out then?"

"Now, that I can't answer," said Denver. " 'Cause nobody's worked off his time yet."

"But this mine has been here a long time, has it not?"

"Sure," said Denver. "Thing is, they only been working it this way, with prisoners, a few months."

Gil said, "Sterne, he had regular miners working it. Then something like six months ago they found out part of the mine was sitting right smack on top of an old Indian burying ground. That changed everything."

"I do not understand."

"One of Sterne's crew turned up the first Indian bones," Denver explained. "That very same day, not more than a couple hours later, as I heard the story, this same miner gets himself killed in some kind of cave-in. That done it. Like opening up a nest of hornets in the middle of a church picnic."

"Within a day," said Gil, "Sterne's whole crew had packed up and hightailed it for elsewhere. They didn't want to work in no hole full of Indian ghosts.

Can't say I blame them none. If I had a choice, I wouldn't, either."

"Not many able-bodied boys left in these parts," Denver said helpfully. "The Lucky Susan Mine here's one of the last producing silver mines. You must of seen what Silver Creek's like, only a few steps away from being a ghost town."

"Sterne and Banner, who's got some kind of partnership in the whole shebang," said Gil, "got them the bright idea of using fellows who was serving time in the Silver Creek jail to work here. That wasn't enough, though, so they took to railroading just about anybody who passed through, or even near, the town. They made them a deal with the sheriff. I guess it was either that or go bankrupt."

Caine shook his head. "Is it not foolish to fear other men's bones?"

"I don't know about that now," said Denver, easing himself down to sit on the edge of Caine's bunk. "They got a saying in these hills. 'Whoever disturbs another man's bones will find his own grave 'fore the sun sets.' You start believing things like that when you see them coming true."

"Those four fellows," said Gil, "who tried to get away. One of them had dug up an Indian's skull that very same day."

"So," said Caine, "we are here as slaves because men are afraid to work here freely."

"That's about the size of it," said Denver. "Like I told you, Caine, there's not no way out. Not alive, leastways." He got up. "It won't help you none to think about it."

Caine, whose eyes were fixed on the night sky

35

beyond the barred window, was silent. When he finally spoke, it seemed as if he were changing the subject. "Has either of you known a man—my half-brother—called Daniel Caine?"

SIX

The train stopped again, with a vast exhalation of steam and a jiggling and swaying that suggested finality, a mile and a half out of Foothill.

Conrad Maine leaped once more from his seat. He was a frail, thin man, wearing a beaver hat and a chocolate-brown suit with a fine gray stripe. His vest, which was made of something that closely resembled silk, was flecked with tiny yellow daisies. The scarlet shade of his string tie was a moderately subdued one. "Mutton-headed ninny," he said, inclining his right hand toward the sooty window of the car.

The train gave a final gasping jerk.

This caused the chubby conductor, who'd been

trotting down the aisle toward Maine, to go toppling backward to the faded flowered carpeting. "Oof," he said.

"Get off your bumpkin and pay attention to me, you buffoon," suggested Maine. He pointed again out the window. "What do you see out there?"

"Oof," repeated the conductor as the second lead man in Maine's acting troupe helped him up. "Beg pardon, sir?"

"We are not," said Maine, "in Foothill."

The conductor buffed his cap brim on his elbow. "We had to stop again—"

"So I surmised."

"Because of the Indians," the conductor finished.

The large handsome actress sitting in the seat behind Maine's gasped. "Are we being attacked by Indians?"

"Oh, no, ma'am," the conductor assured her. "It was only a couple of them sleeping on the tracks. They do that sometimes in these warm spells when—"

"Do you have any notion, you nit, what time it is?" With a slow flourish Maine produced an apparently gold watch from a pocket of his daisy-speckled vest.

The conductor drew out his watch. "Four oh six, sir."

"I make it four eleven."

"Couldn't be that late, sir, because I set mine with the clock at Yountville and—"

"We do both agree that it is well past the hour of four in the afternoon, do we not?"

"Six minutes I wouldn't say is well past, but I—"

"When we boarded this infernal machine, after a highly successful four days in Virginia City, playing to packed and enthusiastic houses with our performances of both *The Spanish Tragedy* and *The Knight of the Burning Pestle,* we were promised by your pickpenny railroading company that we would arrive at Foothill at exactly three oh seven in the afternoon."

"Three oh nine," corrected the conductor. "Three oh nine is when we're due in Foothill. They had that chalked right up, big as life, in the station in Virg—"

"Be that as it may, rum-blossom, it is now well beyond four, and I find myself and my company in the midst of nowhere."

"Oh, this isn't nowhere," explained the conductor. "We're only about a mile or so outside of Foothill."

"And when do you expect we will at long last reach our destination?"

"As soon as they get the driving wheel mended up, we'll—"

"I thought you said we'd stopped merely because of some savages on the tracks?"

"Well, part of the driving wheel fell off when we stopped," the conductor told the actor. "They should, though, sir, have it fixed up in a jiffy."

"We are scheduled," Maine said, his black-circled eyes on the man, "to open tonight in the Foothill Theatrical Palace with our much-lauded production of *The Maid's Tragedy.*"

"Never seen that one."

"I don't imagine you have," said Maine. "Allow me to remind you that if we miss our engagement,

I will bring a colossal lawsuit against not only this rattletrap railroad, but against you personally and all your heirs and assigns unto the fourth generation."

The conductor was about to speak when the train jumped, swayed, snorted, and commenced to roll once again.

Sighing, Maine sank back into his seat, shielding his eyes from the bright afternoon with one thin hand.

Toward the rear of the car a slender, auburn-haired girl also sighed, a less audible sigh.

The heavier blonde girl next to her said, "Relax now, Jenny. We'll be there soon."

"It's these last few miles," said Jenny Warden. "Seems like no time at all since I left home two months ago, but it feels like forever since we left Virginia City."

"You picked a tough way to get where you want to go, traveling with our company," said the blonde.

"It hasn't been so bad," replied Jenny. "The parts, even though they're small, are fun, and I like 'most everybody. I couldn't have, anyway, afforded to come west any other way."

"You pretty sure you'll find him in Foothill?"

Jenny turned her face toward the afternoon outside. "I simply don't know, Belle. It's where he was when he wrote me that last letter. That was over four months ago, I know, but he said he had a good chance for a job in Foothill."

"He didn't say doing what?"

"No, he didn't. He told me it wouldn't take him any time at all to save enough to send for me," said

40

the auburn-haired girl. "That was the last I heard from him."

Belle put her hand on the other girl's. "Well, I've got a feeling he'll be up ahead in Foothill, or close by, anyway." She added teasingly, "If not, you'll find another suitor, the way they cluster around. Maybe Mr. Spider, or Mr. Abel, or Mr.—"

"Stop! You're getting the names all wrong. It was Mr. Speidel, even if he did look something like a spider, and it wasn't Mr. Abel, it was Mr. King— no, that's not right. Now you've got me doing it. Look, I'll be all right once we get there, truly I will."

SEVEN

The lantern flame burned an unearthly blue. The shadows of the working men lengthened and contracted on the blue-black walls of the mine cavern.

Gil stopped working with his drill to wipe sweat from his forehead and bare chest. He gulped in a deep breath. "Don't it bother you down here?"

Caine, who was wielding a pick, answered, "No."

Wiping his face with the back of his hand, the young man said, "You been digging like fury since we started our shift. It don't seem to have fazed you none."

"I do not think about it."

Shaking his head, Gil resumed his drilling. "Just pray we don't come across any Indian bones," he said. "This life here ain't much, but I'm not anxious to cash in yet."

After a few seconds Caine, in his mind, was no longer there beneath the earth. No longer in the mine, no longer breathing the foul air and working in the flickering blue light. He was back in time, back in his own past and again at the Shaolin temple.

It was night, a starless night, and the courtyard was a sooty black. Only faint yellow light from a row of distant candles reached the young Caine where he stood.

Before the lanky boy rose an iron gate. He was halted before it, a look of mingled curiosity and fear touching his face.

After a moment the voice of Master Po came out of the darkness behind him. "Why do you hesitate, grasshopper?"

Caine turned to look at the approaching priest. "I am afraid."

Po stopped beside him. "What is it you fear?"

Reaching out to touch the bars of the iron gate, Caine replied, "I do not know what lies beyond here."

"It is only a corridor. At the end is a room which is no longer in use," the blind priest told him. "Is that something to fear?"

"It is very dark, master."

"Is it not also dark in your room?"

"Yes."

"And do you have fear there, too?"

"No, master."

"Perhaps, then, there is a greater reason for your fear."

Young Caine hesitated, then confided, "Before I came here, a boy who begged in the marketplace told me of a corridor of death. He said the room at the end held the bones of many who had entered and never returned."

A smile appeared on Master Po's face. "But, grasshopper, what is it that I have told you?"

"That life is a corridor," replied Caine, "and death merely a door."

"Do you not believe me?"

"Yes, master," said Caine slowly. "Yet I am still afraid."

The blind priest placed a hand on the boy's shoulder. "In time you will learn to fear only your own fear," he said. "Now your bed awaits you, grasshopper."

"You can stop for a while."

Caine saw Denver standing near him.

The older man said, "We get a ten-minute rest spell now."

"I am not tired."

"Well, most of us are."

Caine looked at him searchingly, then laid aside his pick and seated himself on the rocky cavern floor.

Denver hunkered down beside him. In a low voice, his lips barely moving, he said, "See that big fellow down the tunnel there? Maybe you noticed him in our bunkhouse already?"

"Yes, he never speaks."

"I don't think he maybe can. Anyways, you want to stay clear of him. Name's Hannibal. He's dangerous."

"I have seen him use his strength only against the walls of this mine."

"He can hurt you other ways," said Denver. "He watches everybody . . . and Banner finds out things that way."

"I am doing nothing wrong."

"Yeah, but sooner or later you're going to want to stop, rest for a minute. Or you'll just slow down. Hannibal's going to see that."

"I will rest only if I cannot go on," said Caine. "Until then I will work."

Denver rubbed a knuckle along a weathered cheek. "I don't quite figure you, Caine," he said. "Don't tell me you enjoy being a hopeless slave of Sterne and Banner?"

"The power to hope cannot be taken away from me with a gun or fences."

Denver shook his head. "You'll wind up with a bullet in you, like them four Banner had gunned down."

"To seek freedom a man must struggle," Caine explained. "But to win freedom he must wisely choose where and when he will struggle."

Denver studied him for a moment. "Suit yourself," he said. "I was just trying to help."

"Thank you," Caine said as Denver moved away. Then, taking up his pick, he returned to work.

A moment later a voice said, "Put down that pick, Chinaman."

It was Rupp. He stood a yard from Caine, his

own pick clutched in both hands. "What is it you wish?" Caine asked him.

"I wish to teach you a lesson," growled Rupp. "And I'm going to do it right now." He took an angry step forward.

EIGHT

Rupp's hair glowed blue in the lantern light. He stalked closer to Caine, the handle end of his pick pointing at him. "You got a few things to learn, Chinaman." He gestured angrily at the nearest ore cart, the one it was Caine's job to fill. "What do you think you're doing?"

"I was told to work," replied Caine. "I am working."

Closer still, Rupp said, "Down here, Chinaman, you work the way I tell you."

"What is troubling you?" Caine asked patiently.

"Look at that cart and you'll see." Rupp jabbed the pick handle in the direction of Caine's cart. "You got twice as much ore in yours as any of us others."

Perplexed, Caine waited.

Rupp brought the handle up until it was a foot from Caine's face. "The idea down here is you don't try to show anybody up. You got a minimum quota you got to make every day. So you make it . . . and not one ounce more. Extra work ain't going to get . . ."

Around a bend in the rocky mine corridor someone began whistling.

"Don't forget what I told you."

By the time Banner appeared, Rupp was back swinging his pick.

The big man was carrying a much-worn ledger book in his hand and a stub of a pencil. Halting beside Caine's ore cart, Banner made a notation in the ledger. "Doing pretty good on your first day with us, Caine," he said. "Keep it up and those dimes will start piling up for you."

Caine said nothing and after a few more seconds Banner moved on.

Next to Rupp's cart Banner stopped again. "Funny how a greenhorn Chinaman can dig out more ore than a big strapping lad like you, Rupp."

"Ain't it, though."

"I wouldn't like," said Banner, pressing down harder with his pencil on a new page of the ledger, "to get the idea you and your gang aren't doing all you could, Rupp. A man who can't get the best out of his men don't deserve . . ."

"They're doing the best they can. I keep them going full steam all day. You ought to—"

"See if you can get a little more out of them today," said Banner, moving on. "Maybe we'll have to think about upping your quotas."

When he was out of earshot, Rupp glared over at Caine. "See what you done?"

Caine kept on working. He was used to work, and the discipline of the Shaolin temple had ingrained in him the importance of doing well whatever one did. Now he was dragging silver ore with the same dispatch that he had tried as a boy to bring to sweeping leaves and snow from the temple courtyard, and that later he had brought to the other skills the masters had taught him in his long training for the priesthood.

He was briefly amused when he considered his situation: on two continents posters proclaimed a reward for his capture as the assassin of a member of the Chinese Imperial family, yet here he was imprisoned for a handful of beans. He thought of the scars on his forearms, the emblem of his priesthood. "From the dragon we learn to ride the wind." It was a strange wind Caine was riding now.

It happened at dusk.

The men on the day shift in the mine were coming off. As they moved out of the mine, Denver put an arm on Caine's shoulder. "Got my ankle all scratched up somehow," he said. "Trouble with these dang low-top boots, get all kinds of rocks and gravel in there."

"I am sorry you are hurt."

"Oh, it ain't nothing serious." Denver was limping.

A few more yards, and he slowed even more.

One of the guards, the bearded one, came striding across the plateau toward him. "This ain't no funeral parade, Denver. Get a move on."

"Foot's all bleeding." He stopped completely.

"And no back talk." The guard prodded the older man in the back with his rifle butt.

Denver straightened under the blow, then doubled over. He dropped hard to one knee, hands rubbing at his back.

The guard raised the rifle butt again.

"Let him alone, dang you!" Gil jumped from the line of men, lunged, got himself between the bearded guard and Denver.

Two other guards ran for Gil.

Gil grabbed the stock of the bearded guard's rifle. "You ain't going to hurt him."

"You ought to join in, Chinaman." Rupp came up behind Caine and gave him a vicious shove toward the struggle.

Taken by surprise, Caine went stumbling sideways. He bumped into one of the guards. Both men fell, tangled together. Caine got to his feet and was about to step clear when a rifle butt slammed into his spine, thrusting him forward. Twisting as he fell, he lashed a kick toward the guard who had struck him. The guard dropped.

Beside him another guard had an armlock on Gil and was holding him while the bearded man drove a fist into Gil's stomach. Both droped him simultaneously and grabbed for Caine.

"No," said Caine. Swiftly he took hold of the bearded man's swinging arm, levering him around and away.

While the bearded man was hobbling backward, the guard who had fallen with Caine leaped up and came for him, using his rifle as a club.

Caine gripped the rifle and tossed it, and the man holding it, aside.

"Look out," warned Gil.

Another guard, the freckled Nolan, was in the fight, leaping for Caine's back.

Suddenly Caine was not there.

Nolan grabbed only twilight.

He fell straight down to the ground with a breath-taking thump.

The bearded guard was back, mad, and aiming his rifle at Caine.

Caine's foot whizzed up.

The rifle flew from the bearded man's hands.

Banner said, "That'll be enough, Caine."

Banner had come running from the office building. He had his .44 revolver aimed at Caine, and he was standing a safe ten feet from him. "I don't exactly know what you just done, nor how," he said. "But I ain't going to get close enough to let you try any on me. Take one step and I'll drop you."

Caine stood silently erect, his eyes on Banner's face.

"That was sure something," said Denver, getting himself up off the ground.

"He might of done that to you," one of the men told Rupp.

"Like to see him try," muttered the blond man.

"You were told to cooperate," Banner said to Caine. "Looks like you're going to need a stronger lesson."

51

The bearded guard, who kept blinking his eyes and shaking his head, said, "Wasn't him what started the fracas, Mr. Banner. It was that one." He pointed at Gil.

Gil was standing beside Denver, the hands at his side clenched into fists. "You got no right to knock down—"

"That's enough out of you," said Banner. "Seems like you got to learn you're not in a saloon no more, Gil." He took a step back. "Four days in the Box for Caine and Gil. Get the rest of these men back to their barracks. And, Caine, if you try anything funny I'll gun you and your buddy down right here."

Not waiting for a guard to grab him, Caine walked toward the metal-walled box.

A guard threw open the door. "Out, you." Slowly, scarcely able to stand, the prisoner emerged.

A moment later the door slammed metallically shut. Caine and Gil were inside.

NINE

Banner reached out to touch the office window. It was chill. Nodding at the black night beyond, he said, "Going to be nice and cold tonight. That should make Caine's first night in the Box real interesting for him."

Slouched in his desk chair, arms hanging at his sides, Sterne said, "I don't know about that Chinaman."

"You don't have to know about him," said Banner. "You start thinking about all these crooks and thieves and bums we got working for us and you won't have time for nothing else."

The chunky man let out a long sigh. "Sometimes, Banner," he said, "I can't help thinking that what's been happening . . . that it's, well . . . some kind of judgment."

"A judgment for what?"

"The kind of money that was used to buy this mine," said Sterne, his eyes on the floor. "It wasn't exactly what you'd call clean money."

"You ought to travel more, Sterne," said Banner. "You ought to take yourself a walk through places like Chicago and San Francisco and the like. You'd see men living in palaces, palaces they built on money a whole lot dirtier than anything we ever touched."

After a few seconds Sterne said, "It was blood money. No matter how you try to talk the fact away."

"Let's just forget about that now."

"I'd surely like to forget, Banner. I put a good deal of time into trying to." He shook his head. "But you got to admit . . . all the things that have been going on round here . . . I mean, of all the mines, how come it's ours that's on top of an Indian burying ground?"

"You got to bury them someplace." Banner moved closer to his partner. "I hate to hear you start sounding like them fools we used to have working for us, Johnny. I figured you for having more guts."

"But things have been happening—"

"Things happen in any mine," said Banner. "Especially one we can't afford to shore up proper."

"It's safe enough," said Sterne.

"Okay, now put your mind on something else," Banner told him. "The ore from that new vein looks real good. Next time I go down to Silver Creek, I'll recruit us a few more hands. We're going to do all right."

"If they let us."

"If who lets us?"

"The ghosts, all them Indians down there in the ground."

"Look, Johnny," said Banner. "Ain't it about time you was getting on home for dinner? Get on over to Lucky Susan and forget all about this superstition stuff."

Slowly, gradually, the blond man pushed out of the chair. "That Chinaman," he said, "he's some kind of omen. I just know."

Banner laughed. "In a way, I'm sorry I had to stick him in the Box," he said. "He's a damn good worker." From a trouser pocket he took a dirty fold of notepaper. "Here's what Hannibal has to say on the matter. 'The Chink works real good. Rupp he don't like that. Says he kill him if he don't slow down.'"

Sterne shuffled to the door. "That only sounds like it's going to be more trouble for all of us." He walked out into the cold dark.

The small dining table in the center of the kitchen was bare. No checkered cloth covering it, no dishes, no utensils. Sterne walked slowly around it once. "Now what?" he said.

From the parlor his wife called, "Are you saying something to me, Jonathan?"

"Well, who in the hell you think I was talking to?" he shouted. "Was you planning to serve dinner tonight or not?"

"I didn't know if you were going to come back." She stood in the doorway, a slender woman in her early thirties, with a kind of weary prettiness. "It occurred to me you might sit over in your office all night and sulk."

"We had some trouble with the men this evening, Susan. You know that." Sterne lowered himself into a straight-back chair beside the bare table. "There's this crazy Chinaman . . ."

"I know, I saw him when Banner brought him in."

"Who was you watching, him or Banner?"

"I was looking out through the door, and I saw the both of them." She folded her arms, leaning against the door jamb. "There's no cause to worry about me and . . . and Banner."

"Well, I'm right happy to hear that, Susan," said her husband, "because I got a dozen other items to worry about already."

"Unlike me," she said. "I haven't a care in the world. I'm happy the whole day through, happy as a meadowlark."

"Look," Sterne said, "we ain't none of us happy at present maybe. But, Susan, I tell you we're mighty near to things getting a whole lot better. A few months of mining this new grade ore . . . it'll be the making of us. Then we can—"

"Everything good is always a few months off."

"Is that my fault? Is it really my fault?" He rested one hand on the table top. "I didn't have no more idea than anybody that we was sittin' on top of this redskin graveyard. If we hadn't . . . if those bums who were working for us hadn't of run off scared, we'd be even closer to real success. Susan, you got to understand the setbacks that hit a man ain't always his fault."

"Nothing's ever your fault. Everything simply falls out of the clear blue on you."

"You aren't being fair."

"I'm maybe tired of being fair. And I'm tired of sitting up here on top of this mountain and looking at nothing but this ramshackle house of ours and all these poor scruffy men you're been dragging in to—"

"That wasn't my idea neither. It was Banner who actually come up with that particular notion," said her husband. "I don't know why you don't never put none of the blame on him. Maybe it's on account of you still . . ." He looked away from the slender woman, not finishing.

"I still what?"

"Never mind, let it ride."

"I made my choice, Jonathan," she said to him. "You don't have to throw that up to me."

He said, "Yeah, and you've made choices before. There's nothing says you got to stick with 'em forever."

"Go to hell." She returned to the parlor.

TEN

Gil's head banged again against the low metal ceiling of the dark punishment shack. "Keep forgetting a man can't stand up straight in this place," he said, his voice unsteady. He continued his hunched pacing of the icy room. "Seems like it's getting colder every minute. And it can't be more than midnight yet."

"It is only ten o'clock." Caine was seated on the floor in the darkness, relaxed.

"How can you be sure?"

"I am sure."

"If that's so, then it's going to be one hell of a lot colder in here." He rubbed at his arms and tried a spurt of in-place running. "Nothing seems to help."

He looked toward Caine, whom he could barely make out in the blackness of their cell. "Don't you feel this cold none?"

"I am aware of it."

"You been just sitting there like it makes no never-mind to you at all."

"There is heat in the body," replied Caine. "If I do not move about, I do not waste that heat."

Gil rubbed more briskly at his arms. "What kind of a man are you, anyway, Caine?"

"I am not different from you."

"You might of convinced me of that before I saw you heaving those guards all around," said Gil. "That's sure something I couldn't begin to do. Never seen any man handle himself like you did out there." He paused to take a chattering breath. "You learn how to do that in China?"

"Yes. That and other things of greater importance."

"Like what?"

"To celebrate every man's life in my own."

"I've done that myself, though not exactly the way you mean," said the young man. "Yeah, I've drunk to everyone's health in more saloons and dives than I can count any more." He had stopped pacing, stopped rubbing at himself. "See, I come out here a while back . . . quite a long while, when you come to consider it. My original idea was to get me a good job out here, or some kind of good business of my own, and then I was going to . . . well, that ain't of no importance no more."

"What did you intend?"

"Oh . . . I had a girl, I left this girl back home,

and when I was making good money I was going to send for her," said Gil. He squatted down near Caine. "I used to have her picture in my watch case, but I sold the watch some time back and then I went and lost the picture. Not that you could see her in the dark here, anyway. Pretty girl, real pretty, knew her most of my life back home. Thing is, I couldn't seem to find any kind of decent work to get into anywhere. What jobs I did get, I never seemed to be able to stick with. So I took to drifting, here and there. I was over in Foothill a few months back, and somebody give me the false idea there might be something doing in Silver Creek." He slapped his palms on his knees. "Anyhow, that's how I reached this point, where I've got nothing left to celebrate and nothing to celebrate with."

"When a man has nothing," Caine told him, "it is then he is most able to lift himself up."

"To my way of thinking, it's way too late for anything like that."

"In our dreams the things we wish happen by magic," said Caine. "When we are awake we know that without effort a man can do nothing."

"There's no point to that now."

"Why do you say that?"

" 'Cause I figure we're doomed," answered the young man. "Leastways, I am. If I live through four days in here, I ain't going to make it much beyond . . . There's a curse on this whole mine. Nobody's going to ever leave it alive."

As Caine listened in the darkness he traveled back again in time. Once more he was at the temple, standing before the strange gate.

Blind Master Po was moving toward him, a reassuring smile on his face. He held a lighted candle in his hand. "Now, grasshopper," he said, "let us discover what lies beyond this particular gate." He gave the iron gate a gentle push, which caused it to swing slowly inward. "Come, we will enter."

With some reluctance young Caine said, "Very well, master." He followed the priest into the shadowy corridor the gate was guarding.

Carrying the flickering candle above his head, the master led Caine along the stone flooring.

At the long corridor's end Caine could now see a carved wooden door. On the other side of that door must lie the room he had heard of, the room of death.

"Ah, yes, here it is," said Master Po, stopping.

"What, sir?"

With his staff Po tapped a wooden beam that rested on the floor near the wall. "You will move it to the center of the corridor."

Young Caine worked the long length of wood away from the wall and placed it where the blind priest had suggested. "It is done, master."

"Walk the length of the beam," Master Po told him. "Do not touch the ground until you reach the other end."

Hands held out, Caine stepped up onto the beam. Trying to keep his eyes off the door at the end of the corridor, he made his way along the beam. A little beyond the midpoint he almost lost his balance, but he caught himself in time and finished.

"Very good," said the priest. "Now try it once more, returning back to me."

The second attempt, particularly with his back to the door, was easier.

"That is better," Master Po said when Caine again stood beside him. "We can leave this place, for now." When they were again in the courtyard he added, "Tomorrow, grasshopper, and for the rest of the week, I want you to practice walking the beam."

"May I know why?"

"In the room on the other side of the door," the priest explained, "there is a pool of acid. Once it was used for plating metal ornaments. It serves at present merely to teach each student the importance of balance."

"You mean, master, that the student must make his way across a beam," Caine asked, "while the beam is suspended over the pool of acid?"

"Ah, you have grasped the circumstances of the test perfectly, grasshopper."

"But if a student should lose his balance and fall . . . will he not be consumed by the acid?"

Master Po replied, "It is essential always to keep one's balance, is it not?" He placed a hand momentarily on the young man's shoulder. "I am certain you will survive."

"I will prepare myself, master."

"That is wise, grasshopper."

"It's getting worse," said Gil. "I feel like I'm getting frostbite or something." He was sitting near Caine, shivering, swaying, hugging at himself.

Caine still sat calmly.

"Caine, how in the name of all that's holy can you *stand* this cold?"

62

The question, Caine decided, was a matter of life or death for Gil. With four days to go—the intense cold alternating with a blistering heat that could dry out a man's very bones—Gil might not survive. But discipline was part of Caine's life, and Gil, by his own account, had little experience of it. Could Caine teach him enough—instantly—for him to get through the next four days? He would have to try.

After a moment Caine asked, "Can you trust me?"

"Yeah, sure," answered Gil, "I trust you, but—"

"If your trust is complete, I can help you."

"I don't know . . ."

"I tell you," continued Caine, "you are not within this prison, it is within you. Do you believe that?"

"I guess so, yes." He was shivering less.

"Then you will direct yourself so the instrument of your body can no longer be played upon by either cold or heat," said Caine. "Now seat yourself as I am seated. Good . . . Let all the effort flow out of you. The weight of your body will become less. Less and less, until the body is one with the spirit and until the spirit has not even the weight of a feather, of a breath, of nothing at all . . ."

ELEVEN

The main street of Foothill was five blocks long, running in a not quite straight line, from west to east. At this hour in the afternoon, with some of the midday heat fading, there was considerable activity. The doors of saloons were swinging to and fro; the wooden stretches of sidewalk in front of the general stores and emporiums echoed with footsteps. A buckboard rolled along the dusty street, pursued by three yellow dogs.

Boetticher stood at the west end of Foothill, surveying the town, a faint smile on his lips. He was dressed in his usual black, though these were fresh clothes he'd changed into after his arrival an hour ago. Nodding to himself, he left the front porch of his hotel and moved toward the center of town.

He went on by the first saloon he passed, a run-down place with a wooden carton side patching a smashed window. The next one, calling itself The Pearl Of Foothill, was in better shape. Boetticher entered.

A dozen customers were scattered around the big room. Three were resting against the long polished bar; the others sat at the various tables.

Leaning an elbow on the bar, Boetticher grinned at the bartender.

His grin was not the kind that caused the short gray-haired man to warm to him, but it did make him come right over and ask, "What can I get for you, mister?"

"Whisky'll do."

The gray bartender placed a glass in front of him and poured.

"Hoping," said Boetticher after a few seconds, "to find an old friend of mine."

"We can never have too many friends."

"He's calling himself Giraud. Leonard Giraud."

"Sure," said the bartender, nodding.

After trying his whisky, Boetticher asked, "You know him, huh?"

"Giraud? 'Most everyone knows him."

"That so," said Boetticher with a smile. "Friend-ly fellow, is he?"

"It ain't so much that," answered the bartender. "But Giraud, he's got money in quite a few enter-prises around Foothill."

"Well off, is he?"

"Ought to be."

Boetticher took one more sip of the whisky, then set the glass down at arm's length. "That's rotten stuff, by the way," he said. "Now as to my old friend, Mr. Giraud . . . whereabouts would I be likely to find him?"

"We ain't had no complaints about our liquor."

"I been in San Francisco recently, and I suppose the quality of life out there spoiled me for Foothill's best."

"I admit the whisky ain't as good as Frisco," said the bartender. "But for Foothill it's pretty damn good."

"Which of Mr. Giraud's many thriving businesses would be likely to be getting his attention about now?"

"He'll be at the Foothill Theatrical Palace," said the little gray man.

"That for certain?"

"Sure. A new bunch of actors come to town yesterday. Actors and actresses. When they's new women in town, that's where Giraud'll be."

"He have an office at this theater of his?"

"Big one with one of them tufted velvet couches in it, so I hear."

"Fancy that." Boetticher put a coin on the bar and left.

When the bartender reached for the money, he found himself shivering.

TWELVE

The man known to Foothill as Leonard Giraud pushed back from his broad desk. Crossing to the window of the large second-story room, he drew the curtains shut after a brief look down at the twilight street. Then he lit the oil lamp mounted on the wall, lit the one on his desk, and moved to the purple sofa against the wall. Lowering himself onto it, he took a cigar from his breast pocket and put it in his mouth. He did not light the cigar.

Giraud was a fleshy man in his late thirties. His thinning hair was curly. He bit on the cigar end, his glance turned toward the window he'd just masked.

The door of his office snapped open.

"You, Giraud, are a base archcove," announced

67

Conrad Maine. He halted by the desk, wrapped in a scarlet dressing gown that might have been silk, and pointed a finger at the theater-owner.

"Mr. Maine," said Giraud, smiling at him, "something seems to have upset you."

"Were it not for the fact that I must remain in a comedic mood tonight," said Maine, his accusing finger still pointing, "in order to give the audience my best in this one-time-only performance of *Roister Doister,* I would clout you one, you fawning knark."

"You're perhaps a little nervous before the rising of the curtain, is that it?"

"The Conrad Maine troupe has been touring the length and breadth of this continent for lo, the past seven years," continued the lean actor, "and if there is one steadfast rule I have insisted on, and there are, in fact, several, it is that the theater-owners and personnel are to keep their hands off my actresses."

Standing, Giraud said, "You're referring to the small unfortunate incident with Miss . . . what was her name again?"

"Jenny Warden," said Maine. "You invaded the sanctity of her dressing room, made several guttersnipe suggestions, and—"

"Nothing came of it."

"Only because Belle Ives intruded at a fortuitous moment."

"Well, Mr. Maine, I'm sorry you're unhappy. To be frank with you, the receipts from last night's performance of . . . what was it again?"

"The Maid's Tragedy by the immortal Beaumont and Fletcher."

"It didn't do so very well in terms of what we took in," said Giraud. "So I thought I might get some other form of reward from your little—"

"Enough!" bellowed Maine. "Let me warn you, Giraud, that should any further incidents arise I will have no choice but to curtail the length of our appearance here in Foothill. Which will mean your patrons may well never have a chance to see Conrad Maine in either *The Knight of the Burning Pestle* or *Gammer Gurton's Needle*. You have been warned."

"Let's hope you pull in a few more paying customers with this thing tonight."

With an eloquent snort Maine left the office, slamming the door behind him.

Moving behind his desk, Giraud said to himself, "I'll have to have another talk with that Jenny after the play is over this evening." He picked up his pen and dipped it in his silver inkstand.

The thin column of sooty smoke fuming up out of the glass shield of his desk lamp began to waver. A faint hot wind blew across the room.

Giraud turned toward the window. His mouth opened and the dead cigar dropped out.

"You're doing even better than Kimbel," said Boetticher, stepping in off the balcony. "Or rather Lofton, as he was calling himself."

"You . . . you've seen him?"

Boetticher kept his black-handled revolver trained on the fleshy man behind the desk. "In fact, I was the last person in this world to see him." He moved to the office door and locked it.

"I didn't . . . didn't know he was dead."

"It happened quite recently," said Boetticher, grinning, his back against the door. "Quite unexpectedly, too, from his point of view. I, on the other hand, had been expecting it for a good long while."

"I suppose," said Giraud, "you've got some notion of revenging yourself on us. A boy's idea."

"My main interest is getting back the money you three stole from my brother. Killing you is secondary."

"You killed Kimbel?"

"Very thoroughly."

"There's no need of doing anything like that here," said Giraud. "I'm perfectly willing to give you money. You've got, though, to promise me to clear out then. I won't have you coming back, holding your brother's death over me."

Boetticher laughed. "You're not setting the terms in this deal."

"How much is it you want?"

"Ten thousand dollars."

Giraud gave a slow nod. "Very well."

Boetticher came closer to the man. "First, I want you to talk to me some, Avison."

"What . . . about what?"

"About killing Dan."

"It wasn't me did that. It was Kimbel and Gunther. I was told we were going to steal some money, pure and simple, and not . . ."

The pistol barrel touched his right ear. "I want to know about Gunther. Where is he?"

"I don't know. I ain't seen him since then."

Boetticher's thumb drew back the hammer on the gun. "Think about it some. Figure over to yourself if it's worth a bullet in the brain right now to protect that scum."

Clearing his throat with a dry, quavering sound, Giraud said, "Well . . . well, last I heard he might be in . . . in Silver Creek."

"Silver Creek. That's near here, isn't it?"

"Fifty miles east, in the mountains," answered Giraud. "Used to be quite a place, when all the mines was producing."

"What's Gunther supposed to be doing over there?"

"I hear he's partner in a mine."

"You said the mines wasn't working."

"This . . . this one is about the last one going. It's called the Lucky Susan and Gunther's got himself a half-interest."

"What's his name these days?"

"I'm not sure."

"Make a guess for me."

Giraud told him the name.

Boetticher moved the pistol a few inches away from the man's head. "What did you boys do with Marianne?"

"You got to see Gunther about that."

"He took her with him?"

A smile showed on the fleshy face. "You aren't as smart as you might think," he said. "She wasn't taken—she came along of her own free will."

"What's that supposed to mean?"

"What the hell do you think? It means she was Gunther's woman long before anything ever happened to your brother," said Giraud, still smiling.

71

"It means she was the one who told Gunther about her loving husband having all that cash. She told him where it was hidden, and if Dan hadn't come home unexpected, he might still be alive. Because the original plan was just to take the money and—"

"No, I can't accept that." Boetticher shook his head, backing away from the desk.

"Suit yourself, but it's God's truth."

The lean man shook his head again. "Not Marianne. She couldn't . . ."

Giraud snatched up his inkstand and hurled it straight at Boetticher. Then he ducked behind the desk.

Splashing black, the inkstand hit Boetticher in the chest. He fired his gun.

The shot went slamming into the base of the desk lamp. The lamp hopped, shattered and spilled flame across the desk top.

Giraud bobbed up with a .22 pistol in his hand and fired at Boetticher.

The bullet missed.

Flame went leaping from the desk to the wall hangings and then to the curtains.

Before Giraud could use his little gun again, Boetticher shot him.

The fleshy man collapsed slowly, one leg giving way, then the other. He knelt for a few seconds on the thick rug before toppling sideways into the burning curtains. The flames took hold of him.

Boetticher left him, unlocked the office door, and walked away.

The fire began to grow and spread.

THIRTEEN

After pouring himself a glass of water from the carafe on Sterne's desk, Banner said, "It's getting on to being time."

Sterne blinked, moving aside the page of figures he'd been working over. "Time for what?"

"For letting them two out of that oven out there." He sipped his water slowly.

The late afternoon outside was a bright hazy yellow. The Box sat there looking like something in a mirage.

"You've seen men hauled out of there plenty times before," said the chunky blond Sterne. "This is going to be just like all them other times. If you weren't so all-fired interested in this little show, you could of gone back down into Silver Creek. We still need—"

"Plenty of time for recruiting more men," cut in Banner. "This is more interesting, because I want to be around when that smart Chinaman comes crawling out of the Box, begging for a drink of water. A man like him, he's like a maverick horse that's got to be broke."

There was a knock on the open door. "You sent for me?" asked the guard Nolan.

"Yeah," said Banner. "I want you to hold the night crew back for a bit, don't let them go down into the mine just yet. Make sure all the men, daytime and nighttime, are gathered around the Box when it's opened."

"That's just going to lose us work time," complained Sterne.

"Maybe, but it's going to teach them something," said Banner with a smile. "Namely, that nobody can beat this setup here, not even some magic Chinaman."

Nolan said, " 'Bout time for the day crew to be coming up."

"Get on out there and make sure every one of them has a real good view."

"Don't you worry." Nolan trotted away into the glaring afternoon.

Banner noticed Sterne was back to working with the page of figures. "Come on, Johnny, you got to see this, too."

Sterne bit down on his pen-holder. "I got a funny feeling," he said. "A feeling maybe I ought to stay right here and get all my affairs in order."

"Don't start getting moody," warned his partner. Then he laughed. "But if you do happen to kick off, I'll see to it you get buried right next to a very important Indian. A chief or a med—"

"It's not a joke. And it ain't superstition, either. I just know—"

"Come on outside, Johnny, and watch this evening's entertainment." Banner caught his arm. "I guarantee it'll cheer you up."

Banner slowed as he approached the Box. Passing the yellow-haired Rupp, he said, "Pay attention to what these two boys look like when we drag them out, Rupp. Unless you start getting more work out of the men, it may be your turn to stew next."

"Now, Mr. Banner, you got no call to . . ."

Chuckling, Banner moved on. When he passed Denver he said to him, "Glad to see you're here to welcome your friends back. I understand as how if it hadn't been for you, there wouldn't have been no trouble at all the other day."

The older man met Banner's stare, but said nothing.

"Old boy like you," continued Banner, "I doubt he could last even two days in there . . . Okay, open her up."

Nolan stepped to the metal door of the Box and unlocked it. It gave a rusty whine as he pulled it open.

"Need any help pulling them out?"

"Well, sir . . ." began Nolan, swallowing.

"What's wrong?" Banner went striding forward. "They ain't dead?"

Caine emerged first. Slowly and carefully he stepped free of the Box. He glanced around at the watching group of men, studied the waning daylight of the sky, and then took a deep relaxed breath.

"Hell, now," said Banner.

"Darn, stubbed my toe," said Gil as he came out into the twilight on his own power. He stretched his arms out and yawned. "Think my leg must of gone to sleep from the way I was sitting. Hi, Denver. Hello there, Rupp, how you been?"

"I'll be danged," said Rupp.

Banner frowned at Caine for an instant more, then he turned on his heel and walked back toward the office.

Sterne caught up with him. "This didn't turn out right at all," he said to his partner. "I . . . I had a feeling it wasn't going to."

FOURTEEN

Several of the men circled around Gil while he washed up at one of the water buckets at the back of the barracks. "I don't quite know how to explain it," he was saying.

"What'd you do inside there?" asked Denver.

"Well, I just did exactly what he told me." Gil wiped his face and hands on the cleanest towel he could find.

Rupp's face wore a puzzled scowl. "If it's freezing, you are going to freeze," he insisted. "And if it's hot . . . then you are going to burn up."

"I talked to Frisco a minute yesterday," said one of the men, "and he ain't over yet bein' in the Box."

"You simply can't be four days in the Box," said

Rupp, "and then come traipsing out like nothing happened. I don't care what anybody tells me."

"Well," grinned Gil, "we was."

"Some kind of trick," said the foreman, scratching at his bright yellow hair. "You must of pulled some kind of trick."

"You're absolutely correct, Rupp," Gil told him. "It was a trick, and Caine taught it to me." He walked over to his bunk, and most of the men stayed behind.

Denver trailed along. "This is one of the dangedest things I ever heard of," he said in a low voice. "You honest didn't find some way to get out of there and then hide somewheres till it was time to come out?"

"Nope. We was inside the Box every minute. It . . . it's like I been saying, tough to explain."

"Beats me." Denver, sighing, lowered himself down onto his bunk.

Gil went to Caine, who was standing alone by a dark window. "Caine?"

"Yes, my friend."

"What I done in there," he began, rubbing the sole of one shoe on the floor. "I mean, if I had to go through something like that again . . . and you wasn't there. Could I do it?"

"What do you believe?"

"Well, I sort of feel like I could," answered the young man. "Though, I don't know, I might be too scared."

"Your belief in yourself can overcome any fear."

"Think so?" Gil nodded to himself. "I been thinking, Caine. Being in the Box and all, that's a pretty tough thing to go through. A lot tougher than having some dried-up banker turn you down for a job . . . But I did it, I went through it and came out okay."

"And you have learned something."

"I have, you're right," answered Gil. "For one thing, I figure I don't have to be so much afraid of things. And something else . . . when we was first in there, that first night when it seemed like the night was going to last for always and it was so dang cold. Well, right then I really wanted a drink. Then after you got to talking to me, though, and I got hold of myself . . . I didn't think about wanting a drink no more."

"That is good."

"So I'm figuring I could maybe do better outside. That is, if we ever get out of this place."

"We will get out," Caine promised him.

A cold wind rubbed at the windows of the dark bunkhouse. Thin cold moonlight cut across the sleeping darkness of the place.

Rupp lay awake, thinking.

He'd been the leader here. Maybe some people'd think it wasn't such a great thing, he reflected, but they'd be wrong. Man's in prison, breaking his back for a dime a day if he's lucky, he needs something to hold onto. Well, he'd had something: authority, respect. He said jump, people jumped. And it was slipping away, no question. There was something about Caine from the start that'd been different . . . a different kind of strength. You could tell it, the way he worked, the way he sort of kept to himself, not griping like the rest, not talking daydreams of what he'd do when he got out. Only thing any of them really knew about it, he was looking for a brother —a half-brother—called Daniel Caine. Then, when he came out of the Box like that, like he'd been away on vacation or something, the men had started looking at him like he was the Almighty . . .

With extreme slowness Rupp rolled out of his bunk. He knelt beside it for a moment. The footsteps of the night guard patrolling outside were growing fainter. Rupp eased his hand under the planks of the bed.

His hand came back holding a crude homemade knife. "I've had all of that Chinaman I can stomach," he thought to himself.

Rising up silently, Rupp began to stalk toward Caine's bunk.

The lanky young man's breathing sounded deep and even.

"You're going to go right on sleeping," Rupp said inside his head.

He crouched beside the bunk and raised the knife.

As his hand plunged downward, it was suddenly stopped.

Caine's hand held Rupp's wrist. He twisted, and the foreman's fingers, against his will, sprang open and dropped the knife. Another twist and Rupp himself was stumbling sideways away from the wooden bed.

"Hey—what's going on?" Denver sat up awake as Rupp went staggering by.

Other men were waking, grunting, grumbling, coughing.

Rupp came back, head low, and dived for Caine.

Caine was up out of the bunk and to one side of it. He gripped Rupp's left arm and, using the charging man's own momentum, deflected him.

Rupp's yellow head smashed into the bunkhouse wall. A tin plate fell off a shelf and clanged like a gong on the floor.

On his feet again, the foreman ran, weaving some, to where his knife had fallen. He snatched it up.

Caine watched him for a few seconds, then stretched out again on his bunk.

"Look out," warned Gil. "He's got the knife."

"He will not use it."

Rupp's fingers clutched the knife handle tighter and tighter. Finally he said, "Not this time, Chinaman. But I ain't through with you." He returned to his bed.

"Tail between his legs," said Denver, laughing.

Gil laughed, too, and soon most of the men in the bunkhouse were laughing.

Only Caine and Rupp did not laugh.

FIFTEEN

Jenny Warden touched the powder puff to a spot on her chin, patted her auburn hair, and then leaned back from the dressing-room mirror. "It's going to be an awfully long two days."

"I know," said Belle, who was sharing the small narrow room. She was still wearing her flowered robe, sitting in a wicker chair with her bare feet up on a costume trunk. "Especially with that fat Giraud lurking around."

"Oh, I don't think he's all that dangerous."

"He may be after Maine gets through lecturing him," the blonde woman told her. "Maine tends to get people twice as excited as they were before he

82

talked to them. I don't know whether it's his delivery or his vocabulary."

"It can't be his acting ability."

"Listen, Maine's not half as bad as some of the actors I've traveled with. There was a fellow named Katz, who specialized in Restoration comedy and . . . but that's got nothing much to do with your problems."

Jenny smiled a small smile. "I think maybe my problems are about over."

"You believe what that fellow at the hotel told you?"

"Yes, I'm certain he was telling the truth," said the girl. "And if that's the case, Gil was there as recently as two months or so ago."

"Not as a guest, remember. The clerk said he was sweeping up to earn his meals and sleeping out in the stables behind the hotel."

"I don't care about that," said Jenny. "That's why I want to find him. I know he hasn't written because he's ashamed, because he hasn't been the success he promised me he was going to be. But that doesn't matter."

"Love is okay," said Belle, "but a little money in the bank never hurt anything, either."

"Plenty of time to worry about that when we're older."

With a shrug Belle said, "I been worrying about money since I was eleven." She got up and moved to the wall hook where her costume was hanging. "I still don't feel you ought to get yourself all ready to find this Gil of yours, Jenny. In two months or whatever it is he can have drifted to another dozen towns. I hate to say this, but once a man starts drifting, it's like some kind of sickness that—"

"Gil's in Silver Creek. The hotel clerk said he had a good lead on a job there. I just know he'll still be there."

"Well, maybe so."

"Mr. Maine has promised me that when we end our four-day engagement here I'll have a day free to go—what is it, Belle?"

The big blonde was staring up at the ceiling. "Funny noises coming from upstairs. I thought I heard a pistol go off."

"A pistol?" Jenny left the mirror, pulling her green-striped wrapper tighter around her. "I didn't hear anything."

A moment later Belle's nose wrinkled. "Maybe I didn't hear a gun go off, but I sure as hell know what smoke smells like."

As they watched the wooden ceiling of their dressing room, it began to turn a yellowish brown, and the white paint started to blister.

"My lord," Belle cried, "it's a fire! We've got to warn everybody."

Grabbing her purse from the dressing table, Jenny ran to the door. In the hallway outside, she called out, "Fire! There's a fire upstairs!"

"That's Giraud's office, I think," said Belle. "Fire! Hey, everybody, the joint's on fire."

"What's all this hue and cry?" Maine burst out of his dressing room in the full costume of Ralph Roister Doister.

"Fire, up there." Belle pointed.

"Great bearded demons, so it is." The long thin

actor pivoted and ran along the corridor. "Fire and inferno! Everyone out, quickly. Try to save some of the costumes."

"You think Giraud is still up there?" Jenny asked.

Belle said, "If he is, he'll have to stay there."

They could see the stairway leading to the upper floor of the theater from here. Black sooty smoke was spilling down from above, rolling and tumbling down the wooden steps.

"Let's get ourselves out before this thing falls in on top of us." Belle took hold of Jenny's arm.

The two girls ran down the hallway and toward the rear door of the theater. Belle got there first and hit it with one broad shoulder.

They pushed out into the dark night.

The fire was already noticed. People were stopping at a safe distance, pointing, watching. A file of men, led by a hefty man with a tin star pinned to the watch pocket of his pants, was getting ready to pass buckets of water from a nearby trough.

"They'll never save it," said Belle when they were across the street.

Yellow and orange flames were eating through the upper floor of the Foothill Theatrical Palace. Clouds of black smoke twisted around the carved gingerbread that trimmed the roof. Sparkling red sparks flew upward like plagues of insects.

Conrad Maine came running out of the place, clutching an armful of wigs to his chest. A carpet bag was hung on his arm.

In a few moments all the actors and theater staff were safely out. There was no sign of Giraud.

As the roaring fire took over the entire building,

shaking it, pulling it apart, a tall, lanky man turned away from watching.

It was Boetticher, and he'd been standing a few feet away from Jenny and Belle.

He walked away beyond the crowd and into the night. There was a smile on his face.

SIXTEEN

"You fellows just don't know," said the gaunt bald man as he lowered his pick. "None of you's worked in a mine before."

Working at his usual rapid pace, Caine watched the nearby man out of the corner of his eye.

The gaunt man, whose name was Derby, leaned back against his ore cart as he continued to address the row of working men on either side of him. "But I have worked in them. Matter of fact, I worked in Six Mile Canyon when the Comstock Lode was going strong."

"If you got so damn much experience," said Rupp, "you ought to be able to fill up that cart of yours faster than you been."

"Pay attention to what I'm trying to tell you," said Derby. "I only been here a couple weeks, but I seen plenty enough . . . it ain't no Indian ghosts that're going to kill us all."

"Banner'll do for you if he happens to come strutting by," warned Rupp.

"You ask Mr. Banner next time he pokes his nose down here," said Derby. "He might not admit it, but you'll see in his face that what I say is absolute true."

"What exactly are you getting at?" Denver asked him.

"This mine ain't nowheres near as safe as it should be." Derby gestured at the walls and the timbers. "They ought to shore up the walls a whole hell of a lot better than this. Now when I was working the Comstock Lode they had a system of frames they called square sets, going all the way up the walls. Here in the Lucky Susan, with everybody out to cut corners, you . . ."

Farther down the line Hannibal began to make a frightened croaking sound. His cart gave out a clank as his flung-aside pick hit it.

"What's the matter?" asked Gil.

The mute giant was holding something in his huge fist. Croaking once more, he dropped the object. It was a yellowed bone.

"A grave!" exclaimed Rupp. "Hannibal's dug up a grave!"

"We ought not to dig round here no more," said one of the men. "We ought to get out."

"Bad luck, for sure," murmured Denver.

A guard appeared at the other end of the tunnel. "What's all the ruckus about?"

Waving, Hannibal pointed at the bone.

"An Indian grave," said Rupp. "We shouldn't ought to keep digging hereabouts."

The guard's rifle swung up to point straight at the yellow-haired foreman. "You stay where you are, Rupp," he ordered. "Nobody's going to leave. You all get back to work."

"Not right," said Denver.

"We're smack in the middle of a bunch of Indian dead," Rupp explained to the guard. "This isn't no place to——"

"Making more trouble, Rupp?" Banner was running along the tunnel.

"Not me, no. What's making the trouble is that dead Indian there."

After holstering his pistol Banner walked over to the indicated bone. He picked it up, then laughed. "What's the matter with you? This ain't even a human bone. It's part of some poor old hound dog."

"Never seen a dog with a leg that size," said Derby.

"Well, you seen one now." Banner tossed the bone aside. It shattered against the wall. "Now get back to work." He stalked over to Hannibal.

The giant shook his head, pointing to the fragments of bone.

"Get back to work or I'll shove you in the Box for a whole week, damn you, Hannibal."

Slowly the big man bent and retrieved his pick. After another few seconds he began working again.

"Very good." Banner smiled. "The rest of you get back to work."

Reluctantly the men resumed digging and drilling.

Banner was nearly to the end of the tunnel when the ground began to sway.

The shaft walls seemed to move, to tilt inward. A far-off rumbling commenced, growing louder each second, rolling closer. Everything swayed; the walls seemed to be struggling to hold together.

Then part of one wall came tumbling apart. A support beam toppled, striking the giant Hannibal down. He fell back, reaching toward his injured head.

Black rock and earth fell upon him, nearly engulfing him, slamming him to the tunnel floor.

A minute passed before the men realized the tremor was over, no more of the tunnel was going to give way. They moved again and picked themselves up.

Caine was beside the fallen giant, digging the rubble away from him with his hands. In a moment he had his head and upper chest clear. In another moment he rose up and away from the giant, shaking his head.

"He is dead."

SEVENTEEN

Sterne dropped the Bible into the open grave. "Dang it," he muttered.

Standing beside the wooden coffin that held the remains of Hannibal, Banner signaled Nolan to retrieve it.

"Go down into that fresh-dug grave, you mean?" asked the guard.

"Come on, come on," snapped Banner. "We wasted enough time already digging him out of the mine and getting him crated up."

Reluctantly, Nolan swung a leg over an edge of the newly dug pit. He disappeared for a moment, then came scrambling out with the Bible in his hand.

Banner took it, brushed streaks of earth from the

cover, and thrust it back into Sterne's grasp. "Keep a better hold on it, Johnny. We got no more time to spend on this."

"I'm sorry," said the chunky blond man. "Burying people makes me nervous. I ain't no padre, you know." He began leafing through the book. "Now, where was I when—"

"Read anything. It don't make no difference to this gang of louts."

Watching from a short distance away were the day-shift men, Caine, Gil, Denver, and the rest, with a few of the night men, but most of them had preferred to stay in their bunks.

Sterne wiped his forehead. The hot afternoon sun was making him sweat. After a moment he said, "Here it is. This is what I was reading."

"Get on with it."

" 'Thy rod and Thy staff they comfort me,' " read Sterne.

Rupp shifted his position and went angling over to stand beside one of the other workers. He said something, low and with his lips hardly moving, to the man.

The man's eyebrows went up a fraction; his mouth formed a small o. Then he gave a rapid, furtive nod.

" '. . . Thou preparest a table for me . . .' " went on Sterne. His thick fingers were pressed white on the cover of the Bible, and the book quivered as he read. " '. . . my cup runneth over . . .' "

"You skipped a part," said Nolan.

"Never mind," said Banner. "Keep going."

"I'm not used to reading this kind of printing."

"I know that psalm real well," said the guard.

"My daddy used to recite it when I was no higher than . . ."

"Shut up," ordered Banner. "Finish, Sterne."

" '. . . goodness and mercy shall follow me all the days of my life, and I will dwell in the house of the Lord forever.' "

"Amen," said Banner.

"Amen," mumbled a few of the others.

Banner nodded at two of the guards. "Drop him in the hole."

As the guards began struggling with the ropes wound around the wooden box of a coffin, Banner took a step toward the men.

"All right, boys, get moving," he said. "Because of this little incident you've all lost valuable time. You're going to really have to pick up the pace to make your quotas for today."

Rupp cleared his throat, spit in the dirt. "We're not going back in there."

"What are you talking about?" demanded Banner.

"Just like that . . . we ain't going in there no more."

"It ain't safe," said Derby.

"Whole place is jinxed," said another.

"Indian ghosts going to get us all."

"That's right."

"Don't want to end up like Hannibal."

"Now you listen to me," said Banner, his voice rising. "You men are here for one reason. That's the mine. Once you stop working . . . you ain't no earthly value to anybody. Guards."

Three other guards came forward, two with rifles and one with a shotgun.

"Get back into the mine right now . . . or we're going to start shooting."

The guards raised their weapons.

"Hold off now." Carefully skirting the grave, Sterne joined his partner. "What are you doing, Banner?" he whispered. "We're short-handed as it is. Don't go killing more of them."

"How many times have I got to tell you, Johnny, that you got to leave the discipline to me?" said Banner. "It's better to lose a couple men than to have all of them thinking they can defy me."

Sterne said, "Yes, but . . ."

"No buts about it. We're going to run things around here my way."

The chunky man looked toward the poised weapons, then at the workers. "Well, at least give them a little time to think about it."

Holding up one hand and raising his voice, Banner announced, "It's against my better judgment, but Mr. Sterne insists you men should be given a chance to reconsider. So . . ." He eased his gold pocket watch out of his pocket and tapped its face with two fingers. "You have five minutes. When that five minutes has passed, I'm ordering the guards to start shooting."

Gil had moved beside Caine. "He's bluffing," he said.

Caine was frowning. "I do not think so."

"Five minutes," repeated Banner.

EIGHTEEN

Pine trees rose high all around them, casting stripes of shade across the trail the buckboard was following.

"You handle the team very well," Jenny said to Belle.

"I worked with horses two seasons with a circus once," replied the ample blonde, the reins held casually in her hand. "Drove one of those chariots around the ring. No future in that kind of work."

Jenny watched two jays go fighting up the side of a shaggy pine tree. "Anyway," she said, "some good came out of the fire. Mr. Maine let us take some time off right away, instead of having to wait two more days to go to Silver Creek."

."What else could he do? The Palace burned to the ground, and Giraud along with it apparently."

"I'm sorry about him, even if . . ."

"Forget about him," advised Belle. "Put your mind on pleasanter things."

Jenny smiled. "I have a very strong premonition I'm going to finally find Gil, up ahead in Silver Creek. How much farther is it?"

"We've got a good twenty miles to go." Belle glanced up through the trees at the bright sky. "We'll get there late this afternoon if all goes well. You know, Jenny, maybe . . . oh, skip it."

"No, Belle, what were you going to say?"

"Well, simply this. You maybe ought to prepare yourself in case this Gil of yours might have had some other reason for stopping his correspondence with you."

"What do you mean?"

"It's all very romantic to follow your man halfway 'cross the country. Still, it could be he stopped writing those love letters because . . ."

"No, it's not that, Belle," said Jenny. "I know what you're going to say. That maybe he's met a new girl out here. No, I simply don't believe that."

"Such things happen," said Belle. "Leastways, they happen to me."

"I don't . . ."

One of the horses snorted, then shied.

"What the heck?" exclaimed Belle.

Two men rode out of the wood and onto the trail a dozen yards in front of them.

"Whoa," called out one of the men. He was small and fine-boned, with a large head and deep-set eyes.

His face, beneath a wide-brim gray Stetson, was dotted with pockmarks. No hair seemed to grow on his cheeks or chin.

The buckboard swayed as Belle pulled up on the reins and the horses halted.

"What are you two up to?" she asked the men.

The other one was young, not more than twenty. He had an upturned nose, and his mouth hung always slightly open. His hair was long, a tallowy blond. He wore no hat, had a beaded Indian headband wound tight. His overalls and faded shirt were smeared with dust and dry mud. "Good day, ladies," he said. In each of his dirty, scabby hands he held a Colt .44 revolver.

The other man carried no visible weapons. Touching the brim of his hat with delicate fingers, he said, "Mighty dangerous to travel all alone in these parts."

"You ought," suggested the blond boy, "to have yourselves an escort."

"No, thank you," said Belle. "We don't have that much farther to go."

"Oh, really?" The blond boy giggled.

"Ain't nothing much around here," said his mate. "Right now you're halfway from nowheres."

"You need a pair of gentlemen to protect you from the hazards of the road."

Belle said, "What is it you want?"

"Nothing but to be of service." The little one brought his horse, a muddy roan, up nearer to the buckboard. "But you don't seem to take kindly to our helpful offer."

"It's tough being Samaritans," said the blond boy, riding up to Jenny's side of the wagon. "People nowadays, they don't trust each other. Ain't that right, miss?"

Jenny made no reply.

"That's a handsome portmanteau," remarked the little one, nodding at the back of the wagon. "Probably a lot of interesting, not to mention valuable, things residing in a handsome piece of luggage like that there."

"We don't have much money," Belle told him. "Why don't you wait for the next pilgrim?"

"You got other things besides money." The blond boy, giggling once again, rose up in his stirrups and reached a scabby hand toward Jenny's auburn hair.

There was a crackling, snapping sound.

"Oh, cripes," said the boy. He kept rising until he was standing up in the saddle rigid. His hands came up, as though he were trying to grab at something just behind him. Blood began to come out of him— out of his chest, running down his dusty shirt, spilling over onto the bib of his overalls. He stayed erect for another instant before swinging sideways. His right foot jerked free of the stirrup, but his left foot stayed hooked. He hung from the side of his mount, crumpled in a sharp-edged heap on the ground with one leg sticking up.

"Ride on, friend," said a voice from back on the trail.

"You hadn't ought to've shot him," said the little one. "You killed him, and he wasn't hardly even a man."

The lean man who came riding up was grinning, his black revolver trained on the fragile man. "What was you figuring to do with these ladies after you robbed them?"

"We wasn't aiming to kill them. Only just have some fun."

"Well, maybe gunning down people like you is my idea of fun. So you better throw your friend up into his saddle, then ride away from here fast." Boetticher pointed in the direction he had come, back toward Foothill. "That way."

"I got no plans to go there."

"Yes, as of this moment you truly do."

The little man got his horse to the edge of the trail and dismounted.

"Thank you," Belle told Boetticher. "No telling what they might have done."

Boetticher was watching the little one. "Leave the guns be."

"I was only figuring on sending them home to his people, as a memento."

"Let them lie." He turned, smiling at the two girls. "Glad I came along when I did."

Jenny said, "I appreciate it . . . though I don't believe you had to kill that boy. You could simply have . . ."

"Oh, I could have done any number of different things," grinned Boetticher. "I could even have waited back there until these two were through with you. But I chose to do what I did, and it's over now."

"He's all bloody," complained the little one. "Hefting him up into the saddle, I'm sure to make a mess of myself."

"Do it." Boetticher turned to Belle. "I'm riding as far as Silver Creek. Where you headed for?"

"That's where we're going, Silver Creek."
"Might be a good idea if I rode along with you."
"That'll be fine," Belle told him.
Jenny said nothing.

NINETEEN

"Two minutes," said Banner in a level voice.

The guards assigned to lower Hannibal into his grave had stopped working when Banner had begun counting off time. One of them sat at the grave, his thin legs dangling down into it. The other stood leaning with one palm against the lid of the pine box.

Rupp's yellow hair hung down across his forehead, damp with sweat. He was standing about fifteen feet away from Banner and the men with the guns. "You'll never do it," he said. He pointed at Sterne, who was standing in the shadow of his partner, still holding tight to the Bible. "He ain't going to let you kill us, Banner. Who'd mine his silver for him then?"

"Be more bad luck for the Lucky Susan," called out Derby.

"You'd have to close down."

"Be wiped out, the pair of you."

"Maybe—" began Sterne.

"Shut up," Banner told him without looking at him. "One minute and thirty seconds, gentlemen."

Rupp made an angry growling sound. "You're bluffing, Banner," he shouted. "We're going to call you on it. We're not going back to work."

"Suit yourself. After four or five of you are lying on the ground . . . the rest'll go back to work."

"Bull," said Rupp.

"I guarantee you'll be one of the dead ones, Rupp," Banner promised, patting his holster. "Talk while you can, get what you got to say said."

A silence hit them all then. The defiant workmen stood, unmoving and unspeaking, their eyes on Banner and the armed guards.

Banner casually checked his gold watch. Not saying anything, he held up one finger. Then he reached his six-shooter out of its holster. He was smiling faintly.

Behind him Sterne dropped the Bible again. "Sorry, excuse me."

"He is bluffing, isn't he?" Gil asked Caine.

"Mr. Banner is a man to whom life does not mean much," said Caine. "The silver is very important to him. He will not hesitate to take a life if he believes it will bring the others back to the mine."

"Half a minute left, boys," said Banner. "Better start praying."

"To hell with you, Banner." Rupp reached out

102

and linked arms with the man next to him. "Come on, boys, make a wall."

The linking passed down the line.

"You'll have to gun us all down, Banner," said Rupp.

When the man next to Caine moved to join arms with him, Caine pulled back out of the line. "No," he said.

"Twenty seconds."

Without further word, Caine turned his back on the guns to begin walking across the plateau toward the entrance of the mine.

"Caine!" Rupp bellowed. "Come back here and stand up like a man. Come back!"

"Fifteen seconds."

"You got the only one you're going to get, Banner," said Rupp. "A yellow-skin! That's all you're getting."

Gil let out his breath. "He's got one more," he said softly, turning to follow Caine.

"He beat the Box," said Denver. "Maybe he's got some way to beat that mine." He unlinked his arms and went after his two friends.

"Them Chinese are like Indians," said Derby. "They know things a white man don't." He broke free of the group and headed for the mine.

"Five seconds."

The rest of the men backed, turned, and went, some dragging their feet, walking to the entrance of the Lucky Susan.

"Time's up," said Banner with a smile.

Rupp, who still stood his ground, raised his hands in a gesture of surrender. "Okay, Banner, you win.

This time, anyhow. I'll go back to work along with the rest of them cowards."

"Oh, no, Rupp," said Banner. "You're going into the Box."

Two guards came up to take hold of Rupp.

Banner ordered, "Four days in the Box for him."

"Four days? Nobody can stand four days in that oven," said Rupp.

"You should of asked the Chinaman for some advice. Toss him in."

"I ain't going to forget this," called Rupp as he was hustled away.

Banner laughed. "You sure ain't." He thrust his gun away and gave Sterne a pat on the back. "See, Johnny, I told you they'd do what I wanted them to do."

"We got two less men on the day shift now," replied his partner.

TWENTY

Gil tossed the final shovelful of ore into the cart. "That does her," he said, standing aside to let two other men push the filled cart away on its tracks. He stood up straight and leaned his shovel against the blue-black tunnel wall. He stretched his arms over his head until his bones made crackling sounds. Then he moved to where Caine was working. "Caine?"

Caine looked at him, but kept swinging his pick.

"I've been trying to go over in my head why you did it," Gil said. "Were you afraid of getting killed out there . . . is that why you gave in to Banner?"

Caine lowered the pick. "Is it not wrong to cast life aside for no true purpose?"

"But don't it make you mad to see Banner laughing at you, and Rupp calling you a coward?"

"Should I live my life according to Rupp's views?" Caine asked gently.

Gil was silent for a few seconds. "Maybe it would of been better to let him shoot us," he said finally.

"You have plans now," Caine reminded him. "Things you want to do when you are free of this mine."

"I don't know," said Gil. "When I listen to you I get to hoping . . . but, I don't know, when I'm alone I get to thinking I haven't got a chance." He kicked at the rocky wall. "We're all going to die here anyhow."

"We will not die. We will endure . . . until all of us remember we are men."

"Seems sort of hopeless sometimes. I get to feeling we're going to drop one by one, just like Hannibal."

"The power to claim life lies not in superstition but with destiny," said Caine. "When you bow to superstition, you create a new and unhappy destiny."

Caine left the darkness of the mine, traveling once more to the Shaolin temple and into the past.

Blind Master Po's hand reached for the carved wooden door. He inserted an ornate key in the lock, turned it, and pushed the door open. "We are ready for the test."

With slow steps young Caine followed the saffron-robed priest into the circular room.

"Do you see the plank on which you have been practicing?"

"Yes, master."

Black iron sconces circled the stone wall, each holding a half-dozen burning candles. In the center of the room lay a wide sunken pool. The beam now stretched across it, from rim to rim. Wavering vapors rose up from the liquid in the pool, mixing with the fine white smoke of the flickering candles.

Master Po closed the door. "Watch." He tapped the floor once with his staff before walking straight to the edge of the steaming pool. He thrust out one foot and it touched the beam bridge. "You will see, grasshopper, that it is possible to cross safely."

As Caine looked on, his mouth slightly open, the blind priest stepped out on the narrow beam. He watched Po's feet for a moment, but something in the pool itself caught his eye. It was difficult to make out clearly through the rising vapors. But Caine had the notion it was a skeleton, a human skeleton, he was seeing down in the acid. Someone who had failed the test.

"There, not so very hard."

Young Caine blinked. Master Po was on the other side of the pool.

"Now it is your turn."

"Yes, master," answered Caine, not moving.

"Why do you delay, grasshopper?"

"I thought I saw . . ." His horrified voice trailed off.

Po waited. Finally the boy continued, "I see where others have fallen."

"Let your eyes see only the beam," Po advised. "In that way, you will not fall."

Caine made himself walk to the rim of the pool.

107

He swallowed, licking his lips, and stepped onto the beam.

The vapors made the very narrow bridge seem to curve. When Caine was out over the center of the pool he glanced down to get a better look at what he'd seen from the edge. It was a skeleton.

He missed the beam with his next step. For what seemed a long while he hung in the air, tilted over at an impossible angle. He grabbed, but there were nothing but white fumes around.

Caine fell, screaming, down toward the pool's surface.

He felt this was the last moment of his life.

With a giant splash he went under.

He sank several feet before he realized nothing was happening to him. His flesh remained on his bones.

He began swimming, fighting to the air above.

Master Po's laughter filled the room. He held out his staff to the spluttering child. "What is this, grasshopper? You are not yet a pile of bones."

Catching hold of the staff and pulling himself free of the pool, Caine said, "The pool is filled with water, nothing more than warm water."

"Ah, but you believed it was acid."

Shaking himself, scattering flecks of water, he said, "I did see a skeleton, master."

"Did you?" Squatting, Master Po fished in the pool with the end of his staff. "Ah, this must be our horror now." He pulled a man-size length of oilcloth from the water. "An excellent painting, I am told, but only a painting."

Smiling, Caine plucked the painting off the tip of the staff and rolled it up.

"Superstition," Master Po told him, "is like a magnet. It pulls you in the direction of your belief. Having learned that, what is it you fear now?"

"Only my own fear, master."

"Let us return to the courtyard, grasshopper."

"Wonder what he's doing down here?" said Gil.

Caine, who was now shoveling ore into his cart, turned his head to glance in the direction Gil had nodded.

The blond chunky Sterne was down at the end of the tunnel. When he realized Caine was looking at him, Sterne gave a small nod and backed away and out of sight.

"Maybe he's worried," said Gil.

"Worried about his mine," mused Caine, "or about me?"

"Huh?"

TWENTY-ONE

The sound of the metal door opening made Banner jump up and run to the office window. He squinted in his effort to make out what was going on out there in the twilight. "What are those guards up to?" He headed for the door.

"Hold off now, Banner," said his partner.

"They just let Rupp out of the Box. Who told them to do that?"

"I did," answered Sterne. He rocked slightly in his desk chair, locking his hands over his stomach.

"Where do you get off countermanding my orders?" Banner's voice was loud, angry. "I work hard drilling discipline into this shabby gang of misfits we have to work with, and you come along—"

"Rupp is a leader. I think we need him."

Banner stalked over to the desk, grabbed up a handful of papers, and shook them in Sterne's face. "Look at these production figures. There's a boost in tonnage. If we maintain this level another three months we'll own the mine, free and clear."

"Exactly," said Sterne. "And that's why I had them spring Rupp while he's still in shape to do us some good."

"I don't need Rupp to keep production going strong. But I do need some kind of discipline," Banner told him. "You letting him loose . . . that'll make them think a man can defy me and get away with it."

"Sometimes you let your pride get in the way of your common sense."

"Don't start giving me preacher talk, Johnny."

"I'll tell you," said Sterne. "I've worked with men as much as you have. Even did a stretch in the army. I've seen what can happen to men when a real leader comes down the pike."

"You mean Caine?"

"I surely do mean Caine."

"But I broke his spirit," said Banner. "Maybe he outfoxed me by coming out of the Box all spry . . . but when it came to a showdown, he didn't have the guts to stand up to me."

Shaking his head, Sterne said, "I been thinking about that. What I come to conclude is that Caine knew the men weren't ready. Any hot-headed heroics on the spot we would of dealt with with guns. But if he gets to working on those men, giving them hope

111

and dignity, if he teaches them to be patient and not move against us till the time is ripe . . ."

"There ain't going to be no right time for that."

"Anybody, even a highfalutin king on his throne, can be toppled," said Sterne. "Now the main trouble with Caine is . . . he's got no fear in him. I been watching him. You can see it in his eyes, in the way he carries himself. You're never going to control him, no matter what you try. And if he ain't stopped, he's going to pass some of what he knows on to the rest of them."

Banner paced. "I thought you was scared, getting hunches we was in for bad times? Now—"

"Now I realize it's Caine who's been making me feel this way. With him out of the way . . . I know everything's going to go good for us again."

"All this thinking you been doing, you come up with an idea on how to solve our problem with Caine?"

"Yeah," answered Sterne. "We got to do two things. We got to throw a little fear into the men and—"

"Fear is what almost ruined us in the first place."

"We need it now, trust me," said Sterne. "So we're going to make them really believe the superstition about the Lucky Susan. That means you're going to have to get rid of Caine in a particular way." With a smile on his chunky face, Sterne explained it all to Banner.

The slim, dark-haired Susan came into the little parlor and lit the table lamp. "Or do you prefer to sulk in the dark?"

In his chair Sterne blinked as the yellow light hit him. "Sometimes I wish I was more like Banner," he said to his wife.

"You got that on your mind again?" she said. "I told you, and sometimes now it's hard to see why, I made my choice. I could have stayed with him, but I didn't."

Shaking his head, Sterne said, "It ain't that. I took you from him, that's settled. I know you ain't as happy about it as you used to be, but that can't be helped now. Maybe when . . . anyway, it just seems to me it's easier for Banner to do things that have to be done."

"What has to be done now?"

"We're going to have big trouble with the men unless . . ."

"Unless what?"

"Somebody's got to be taken care of."

"Oh, yes, and you know Banner's good at that." Susan moved back into the shadows beyond the table. "Because he killed my husband, back when we all had different names."

"I wasn't trying to remind you about that," said Sterne. "That's all over and done, like I told you. Whatever you and him done . . ."

"It was never my intention Dan would get killed," said the woman. "But I think maybe Banner was planning that all along. After it happened . . . I went with him anyway. There didn't seem to be anything else to do. Until I met you . . ."

"And that doesn't seem to be too good an idea to you any more," said Sterne. "I know. The only thing I can say is . . . things are going to get better."

"Soon as you have a few more men killed."

"Only one, Susan. Only one."

She laughed. A dry, cold laugh, her face hidden in darkness.

TWENTY-TWO

The day ended, but the heat remained. The desolate streets of Silver Creek were thick with a steamy sort of warmth. Down at the other end of town a dog barked, unseen, hidden in darkness.

"Not what you'd call a thriving community," said Belle as their buckboard entered the town.

"There should be lights," said Jenny, half rising from her seat, staring at the dark buildings that surrounded them.

"You have a specific place in town you're looking for?" asked Boetticher. His black clothes blended with the night so that only his face showed, floating in the air and grinning.

"Not exactly," answered Belle. "Though maybe . . ."

"We'll be all right now, Mr. Boetticher," said Jenny. "You can go on about your own business."

"Don't you think he could help us—"

"No, never mind, Belle. I'd rather we—"

"Be glad to give you any further assistance I can."

"No, thank you," said Jenny. "We appreciate what you've done for us, though."

Boetticher's grin widened. "Well, I wish you luck, Miss Warden, and Miss Ives. Evening to you." He gently spurred his horse on along the night street.

Two blocks farther on, he saw a glowing window. He reined up, dismounted, and tethered his horse next to a piebald mare.

There was no door, only a narrow doorway.

Boetticher walked into the narrow saloon. "Good evening, Mr. Estling."

The saloon-keeper raised his pale, lumpy face. "I know you?"

"This is the start of our friendship, Estling. You got your name smeared up on the window, and I noticed it."

The only customer was the black cowboy, Mac-Tell. He had one elbow resting on his table and was pushing his harmonica back and forth through a spill of whisky. "He looks too mean to try nothin' with," he advised Estling.

"What you drinking?" Estling asked.

"Whisky." Boetticher approached the small bar counter. "I'll tell you why I'm here, Estling."

"If you're here for anything besides whisky you're in for a disappointment."

116

"I hope not." Boetticher grinned across at the dough-faced man. "See, I've traveled many a weary mile to have a reunion with an old and valued friend of mine."

Estling poured a shot, set it down. "So?"

"This friend of mine operates a mine," continued Boetticher. "But before I travel on up there, I wanted to make sure he wasn't here in town."

"Who's this friend?" asked MacTell.

Boetticher said, "He calls himself Banner."

"I didn't figure him for having no friends."

"Isn't Banner highly thought of in the community?"

MacTell chuckled. "This here's about all the community Silver Creek's got left," he said. "You maybe ought to think twice about looking up Banner. The way things been going, he's likely to put a pick in your hands and stick you in the mine."

"Having himself some trouble finding able-bodied workmen, is he?"

"No, it ain't no trouble. No trouble for him, though some of the poor jerks he railroads do . . ."

"That's enough," said Estling. "Banner don't want his business talked about all over the place."

Boetticher crossed with his drink and took the chair opposite the black cowboy. "I'd think, with the rest of the mines in the shape I hear they're in, that fellows would be lining up to get work with the only one still going strong."

"They would," said MacTell, "if it weren't for the ghosts . . . seems like miners just can't stand working with ghosts."

117

"Haunted, is it, the Lucky Susan?"

"Turns out it used to be an Indian graveyard up there, and . . ."

"You really asking for it," Estling told the Negro. "Banner hears how you been giving away all his secrets, you're going to end up down in the mine yourself."

"Nope, he's not about to mess with me. I'm a bigger hoodoo than any dead Indian he ever met."

"And Banner," asked Boetticher, "is he up at the mine right now?"

"Far as I know. He ain't been down to town for a few days. Might be he's too busy fighting off ghosts."

"We don't serve no ladies here," Estling announced in a loud voice.

Looking toward the doorway, Boetticher saw Belle standing there. "Evening, miss." He got up and tipped his black sombrero.

Belle motioned him to approach her. "There doesn't seem to be much of anybody in this town," she told him when he was beside her.

"You hunting for some special person?"

Nodding toward the buckboard where Jenny was waiting, Belle said, "She's hoping to find a friend of hers, or at least get some news of him. Could you maybe see if they know him here?"

"That all right with her?"

The blonde nodded. "Has to be, she's got no other choice for getting help," she said. "Your killing that boy back there . . . it upset her quite a lot."

"One time it would have . . . okay, what's the name of this fellow she's looking for?"

"Gil Conselman, tow-headed boy in his twenties. He's supposed to have come here a few months back with some kind of job in view."

"I got a hunch what kind of job he maybe ended up with," said Boetticher. "You wait out in the wagon, miss. I'll find out about him."

"You traveling with them ladies?" asked MacTell. "What kind of business did you say . . . ?"

"You know pretty much everything goes on in Silver Creek." Boetticher was standing over him.

"Ain't all that much going on, but what does, yeah, I know."

"A boy name of Gil Conselman hit town a while back. Know what's become of him?"

"You done asked enough questions for tonight," advised Estling. "I think . . ."

All at once Boetticher's revolver was in his hand, pointing at the saloon-keeper. "Devote yourself to tidying up your establishment, Estling."

The black cowboy cleared his throat and sat up straighter. "Blond kid," he said. "I remember a Gil somebody . . . they made up a charge against him, something about starting a brawl in here. Sentenced him to a year."

"But not in jail, huh?"

"No, up to the mine, the Lucky Susan," replied MacTell. "That's how they can keep it working."

"He should still be up there, then."

"If he's still alive."

"We'll find out." Boetticher holstered his gun. He left the saloon and walked over to the waiting buckboard.

TWENTY-THREE

"Oh, those were the good-time days," said Derby. "Now you take Leadville back in the Sixties, right after old Abe Lee made his strike down in California Gulch. That was some wide-open town, I mean to tell you. There wasn't nothing you couldn't get in Leadville, absolutely nothing. They had a bordello there where the ceiling of it—"

"Cut out the jawing," warned Rupp from down the line. "Banner is down on me already. I don't need you slowing things even more."

"Never had no trouble talking and working," said Derby as he swung his pick.

"What about that ceiling?" asked the husky man working next to him.

"Well, sir," resumed Derby, "that ceiling now. See, this particular business enterprise belonged to a fellow name of Goedewaagen, a Dutchman he was. For a time he run the Left-Handed Dutchman Mine. Then Goedewaagen realized he could do a whole lot better for himself in bordellos, seeing as how the Left-Handed Dutchman was never a topnotch mine. Well, sir, this particular bordello I'm alluding to had itself a ceiling . . ."

"Shut up," said Rupp. "Else I'm coming over and bust this pick handle over your skull."

"Something about bordellos upset you, Rupp?" Derby asked. "I figure after being cooped up here so long, you'd enjoy hearing about a few fancy ladies. Course, your interests may lie in some other direction, and in that case—"

"I told you . . ." Rupp charged down the tunnel. He raised the pick handle to swing it at Derby.

Then he was no longer holding the pick.

"It helps nothing to fight among ourselves," Caine told the yellow-haired foreman. He had stepped out of the line and caught the pick away from the attacking Rupp.

Rupp glowered. "Look, Chinaman, stop telling me what I can and can't do."

Caine silently offered the tool to Rupp.

Around a bend, whistling started.

"I still owe you." The foreman returned to work.

The husky man said to Derby, "About that ceiling?"

"Had it shipped in all the way from Paris, France, around the Cape," replied Derby. "It was all made out of mirrors, you understand, dozens of them."

121

Banner was in the tunnel with them. "Gil," he said, "I'd like you and Caine to work in that cutout over there for a spell." He pointed to an alcove off the tunnel. It was large enough to accommodate two men working.

After Caine and the young man had shifted, Banner continued on down the line. "I'm surprised at you, Derby," he said. He tapped one booted foot on the cart track. "An old-time miner like yourself . . . you ought to be digging out more ore for us."

"Something about the Lucky Susan don't inspire me."

"Sure hope you come to change your mind. Be a shame to have to lock our one real miner up in the Box." He moved on, stopping next by Rupp. "You being back isn't my idea, you know, Rupp."

"Yeah, I figured as much."

"Mr. Sterne seems to think you're capable of continuing as foreman," said Banner. "I must say I haven't seen much evidence of that so far this morning. If anything, production looks to be down from what it was yesterday while you were cooking in the Box."

"Don't blame me. It's that Chinaman and that windy Derby and . . ."

"A foreman, Rupp, a *good* foreman, anyhow, has to be able to get the work out of his men." Banner brought out his ledger book and made a pencil notation. "You got Mr. Sterne on your side for now, but it ain't going to last forever."

"But I—"

"Save your excuses for him. What I want out of you and your men is an honest—"

122

"Cripes, another one!" cried out the husky man.

A faint smile came and went on Banner's face as he turned. "What's the matter?"

"The Chinaman." The husky man gestured at the alcove. "He done dug up another dead Indian."

Gil was standing outside the cutout, watching the kneeling Caine.

Carefully, Caine lifted a human skull up from the dirt.

"What have you got there, Caine?" asked Banner.

Standing up with the skull and a rib bone in his hands, Caine said, "These were in the earth. I will return them to the earth when the digging is done for today." He carried the bones along the tunnel and gently placed them in a place where no work was going on.

"Going to be more bad luck coming," said one of the men.

"Same like happened to Hannibal."

"Ain't right."

Banner told them, "Take a look at the Chinaman. He's not at all scared by the superstition." He closed his book and slipped it away under his coat. "Maybe you men can learn something from him."

"I wouldn't touch them bones for nothing."

"Especially that skull."

When Caine returned to the cutout, Banner said, his voice low, "No use working this spot for the time being. It might make the men uneasy, case you unearth more of them bones. Tell you what, you and Gil start working that new tunnel that runs off this one."

"That ain't shored up proper," said Derby, who'd overheard.

"Of course it is. Old age has made you too cautious, Derby."

Nodding, Caine moved along the main tunnel and stepped into the low tunnel that branched off it.

Gil followed, saying, "Wonder if Derby's right."

Caine frowned, but didn't answer.

Banner watched the rest of the men work for a few moments. Then, casually, he walked along deeper into the main tunnel. When he was out of sight of the men he began trotting. A hundred feet farther on, a natural gallery broke into the tunnel.

Banner hurried into the gallery, after pausing on the threshold to light a candle. The gallery looped back, and when he reached the far wall he could hear the sound of digging quite clearly.

Coiled on the earthen floor was a length of yellow rope. Tipping the candle and spilling wax, Banner fixed it at shoulder height to an outcropping of rock. He bent, took hold of the end of the rope, and began gathering it around his arm. Its other end ran through a jagged crevice in the gallery wall. Banner had set all this up last night. The rope passed over a pulley secured in the crevice, then was wound around a beam in the ceiling of the offshoot tunnel where Caine and Gil were working.

Last night the support beam had been nearly sawed through in two places. When the rope was pulled tight enough, if all went as planned, the weakened section of beam would come out and the ceiling of the little side tunnel would collapse. That should bury Caine and Gil quite effectively.

Banner hated to lose Gil, who was turning into a good worker. But the accident would look more believable if both men perished in it.

Smiling, he gave the rope a ferocious pull.

TWENTY-FOUR

Sterne had been trying not to look toward the mine. He was leaning against the rail of the small porch that fronted his house, sipping coffee from a heavy mug. The morning heat was pressing in on him. He cradled the warm mug in both palms and blew his breath out of his mouth and over his upper lip. He gritted his teeth, sighed, drank at the hot coffee again.

"It's going to happen today, isn't it?" Susan was just inside the open doorway.

"What's going to happen today? What do you mean?"

"I mean you and Banner are going to do it today, your necessary killing."

"Forget about that, Susan," her husband told her. "Anyway, I'm not . . . I won't be . . . hurting anyone."

"Banner's doing it, doing the actual killing," said the woman. "I realize that. Is it going to happen in the mine?"

"No. What makes you think that?"

"You've been avoiding going near the mine this morning, or even to your office," she said. "Usually you can't get out of here, and away from me, fast enough."

"I don't try to avoid you. It's simply that . . . well, the way things have been going, there's a lot of extra work. Very little time for . . ."

"The Chinese boy, is he the one Banner's going to kill?"

Staring into his coffee cup, the chunky Sterne said, "No good comes of dwelling on these things. Anyway, my lord, Susan . . . why do you think I have to get involved in . . . in all this? So the mine'll keep going, so we'll have enough money to live somewhere else. Live the way we want. I . . . these things are done for you as well as for me."

She laughed. "Yes, I know, Jonathan. I've heard all the excuses. From you, from Banner before you. It all comes down to me being the cause of other people dying."

"One Chinaman," said Sterne. "That's not like . . . good lord!"

The whole plateau had begun to shake, the ground to rumble.

Their little wooden house rattled, the windows chattering in their frames, the open door flapping.

Susan ran out onto the porch. "The mine, Jonathan! Something's happened to the mine."

Coffee splashed out of the mug and all over the front of Sterne as he bounded down the steps. Realizing that, finally, he flung the half-full cup from him.

A gigantic rumbling was coming from the direction of the mine.

When Sterne came in sight of the entrance, he saw clouds of dust barreling out into the morning. The ground was still shaking.

Susan caught up with him. "This is because of Banner, isn't it?" she asked, grabbing his arm. "Something he was supposed to do to hurt the Chinese boy."

His eyes on the ruined tunnel entrance, Sterne said in a distant voice, "He wasn't supposed to do this."

Nolan jumped out of his bunk in the guard's barracks. "The mine!" he cried as he dived out the door.

Two other guards came tumbling after him.

Out of the night-shift bunkhouse popped one of the workmen wearing a yellowed suit of long-johns and a Stetson with the front brim tucked back. "It done caved in!"

All the tremors had ceased. The thick billows of dust were no longer pouring out of the tunnel.

Nolan trotted up to Sterne's side. "Looks awful bad, don't it?"

Sterne nodded.

The mouth of the access tunnel to the mine was completely blocked, filled with rubble.

Some of the other night-shift men were coming

out into the hot daylight. "The Indian curse," said one of them. "There's a curse on the mine."

"Rupp was dead right. I hear he told them nobody should go back down there."

"You can't mess with them Indian spirits and expect nothing to go wrong."

"Must all be dead in there."

"Dead or dying."

"No, I bet they got a chance."

"What do you intend to do?" Susan asked her husband.

He was staring at the ton of rock that filled the tunnel mouth. "Well," he said finally, "I suppose there's a chance they're still alive in there."

"Sure, they're down in one of the other tunnels," said one of the night men. "Might be only this tunnel caved in."

"Even if it is only this one," Nolan pointed out, "that means something like seventy-five feet of rock and ore between us and them."

The workman said, "Might be less."

"Might just as easy be more, too."

Susan told Sterne, "You'll have to try."

"Yes, I know." He motioned to Nolan. "Break out the extra tools, picks, and shovels. Rouse up any of the night boys who ain't here, all the guards, even the cook if you need him. Then set everybody to start clearing the tunnel."

"Think we ought to divide the men into groups, let them tackle it in shifts?" asked Nolan.

"See what's called for," said Sterne, "but get going."

Nolan trotted off.

"Air," said Susan. "Are they going to have enough air to breathe down there until we can dig through to them?"

He shook his head. "Probably not."

TWENTY-FIVE

Caine had looked up seconds before it happened.

He saw the shadowy blue-black ceiling of the tunnel begin to quiver. "Away," he said, catching hold of Gil, pulling him toward the larger tunnel.

"What the hell's wrong?"

Caine threw himself, carrying the young man with him, out through the entrance of the side tunnel.

Back where they had been, the ceiling fell.

It came roaring down, a cascade of rock and dust, falling and slamming to the floor.

All of the world above them seemed to be thundering down into the narrow tunnel.

"Cave-in!" shouted Derby. "Roof's falling in."

"Cave-in!"

"Cave-in!"

Caine and Gil rolled to a stop against the wall of the larger tunnel.

The ground continued to shake, the walls to throb.

"Ain't over yet," warned Derby.

From around the bend in the tunnel a man shouted, "Good lord almighty!"

A new roaring began, greater than the first. The sound was like a giant waterfall, like a stampede of buffaloes. Everything above seemed to be coming down.

"Spread," said Derby. "Spreading over to the access tunnel. That's what's caving in now."

"Going to come down on us next." Rupp had his head cocked, his hands hovering near his head.

No one realized for several seconds that silence had come.

"Maybe our tunnel's going to hold." Denver had been backed against the wall, one hand pressed against it.

Rupp started down the tunnel. "What's it like up there?" he called out.

A bearded man came limping around the bend. "Access tunnel's caved in."

"That means . . ."

"Means we're bottled up."

Denver asked, "Take any of your boys with it?"

"Nope, we was able to get back out of the way in time." He scratched dust out of his beard. "Don't know that's going to do us much good in the long run."

"Looks like we're trapped down here," said Rupp.

"Just like Hannibal in his pine box, in the ground with dirt on top of us."

"Only it ain't six feet of earth," said Denver.

"What you figure?" Rupp asked the bearded man. "How much dirt and rock between us and outside?"

"Well, if you want to look on the bright side . . . let's call it sixty-five feet. I'd calculate that's about how much of the tunnel is completely closed up."

Caine, who had helped Gil to his feet, was dusting himself off.

"Thanks for dragging me out," said the young man. "Funny how the whole shebang started right where we was working. I guess Derby sure was right."

Frowning, Caine said, "I am not certain of that."

"What do you mean?"

"I had a fleeting impression I saw a rope attached to one of the ceiling beams in our little tunnel," answered Caine. "A moment before the cave-in, that beam was pulled out of place."

"But . . . but that'd mean this whole thing was on purpose. You can't tell me they want to bury us all down here."

"No, not all of us," said Caine.

Gil thought for a moment. "Somebody only wanted to kill me and you?"

Caine nodded. "To kill me, at least," he said. "It is very important to Mr. Banner that he always win."

"And he sure didn't win out by putting you in the Box." Gil rubbed at his arm. "Still, though, you give in about coming back to work after Rupp tried his showdown."

"I think Banner saw . . ." Caine stopped, turning his head. "Listen."

"Another cave-in?"

"No, I hear someone."

"Coming to rescue us?"

"No, it is from down this way." He hurried along the tunnel, head slightly bent as he listened.

"Help me," came a faint voice from up ahead.

"Sounds like Banner," said Gil.

Caine halted at the entryway to the gallery that branched off the tunnel. He surveyed the darkness within. "There has been a partial cave-in here, too."

"Is that somebody?" Banner's voice was dim. "Help me, I'm pinned in here."

"Might be another trap," cautioned Gil.

"I do not think so." Caine went into the gallery.

"Over here," said Banner in the dark. "I think I busted a couple of my ribs. And my insides don't feel so . . ."

"Do not talk further," Caine told him. "I have found you."

He knelt and began to dig. The rope was still wound around Banner's wrist.

TWENTY-SIX

The bald old Derby squinted down at Banner. "I'm wondering," he said.

Banner was stretched out on the floor of the tunnel, his head resting on his rolled-up coat. A lantern hung on an outcropping of rock two feet above him. "It's bad, isn't it?"

Caine finished examining the injured man. "There are three broken ribs," he said. "And your left leg is broken."

"I can't feel that at all," said Banner. "Not the leg at all. The ribs hurt like hell." He watched Caine's face. "That isn't all that's wrong, is it?"

"I fear there may be internal injuries."

"I'm going to die."

"I did not say that. We still have hope," Caine told him. "We will get out of here and then summon a doctor for you. Meanwhile, I have a few herbs with me which may—"

"A doctor?" said Banner. "We ain't got no camp doctor, you know. There ain't even a sawbones down to Silver Creek any more. You got to send all the way to Foothill for a doctor. By the time—"

"You must not stop hoping."

Banner said, "Might as well let me die, Caine. That's what I had planned for you, you . . ."

"There is no need to talk of that now."

"Ha," said Derby, "that's what I been wondering. Seemed like our cave—"

Rising quickly, Caine placed a hand on the old man's arm. "Do not say any more."

"But they all ought to know what—"

"We must all concentrate on surviving what has happened to us. Not on placing blame."

"When he admits to trying to kill you and to probably starting the whole . . . ?"

Caine increased the pressure on Derby's arm. "Enough. It is best to be silent."

"Caine knows what he's talking about," Gil said.

Several yards away, the rest of the trapped men were gathered around Rupp.

Denver was squatted down, a torn piece of paper on his knee. He was making some calculations with a borrowed pencil. "You got to understand, I'm pretty rusty on this kind of figuring . . . but this is how it looks to me. I'd guess we got enough air down here to last us till about six A.M. tomorrow, give or take an hour."

136

"You take an hour," said Rupp, "and that means we'll all be dead and gone by five."

"Some air now might find its way in from other tunnels or galleries," said Denver. "And, like I say, my figuring may be a little off."

"Okay, okay," said Rupp. "No use kidding ourselves, we'll take the worst-sounding guess. Five tomorrow morning. Now the next question is . . . how long is it going to take them to dig us out of here from up there?"

"Providing they intend to," said one of the others.

"They'll come for us," said Banner in a weak voice. "Sterne's not inhuman."

"That's right," said Rupp. "He ain't quite as bad as you, Banner. If you was out there and him down here with us . . . I'd say our chances would be even worse."

Denver came over to Banner. "How long you figure it will take for them to dig through to us?"

"Won't be no earlier," said Banner, "than tomorrow morning."

"That's what I was figuring."

Rupp gave a bitter laugh. "Going to be a real contest," he said. "The boys up there racing against our supply of air. Anybody care to bet on the outcome?"

"We maybe got more air than we figure," said Denver. "And they might dig down close enough to feed us in some air a lot sooner than tomorrow morning."

"You're starting to talk like your Chinaman friend," said Rupp. "Well, I ain't going to stand around with my thumb on my butt till I choke. Let's start digging, ourselves." He grabbed up a pick.

"Wait," said Caine. "Will not our labor exhaust the supply of air more swiftly?"

"He's right." Banner tried to rise up on an elbow and, painfully, failed.

"So what? At least this way we can die trying."

Gil said, "Listen, he's trying to tell you we don't have to die at all."

"When your eyes start popping out, and your windpipe's drier than sand," said Rupp, "you remember that."

Denver said, "Caine's the only man so far knew how to beat the Box. We ought to pay attention to him."

"Is it not better to remain still," Caine asked, "to burn but one lantern, and free the mind of anxiety?"

Nodding, Gil lowered himself to the tunnel floor. "We just got to wait."

"Wait?" said Rupp. "I don't even know what we're waiting for! Waiting to die?"

"Waiting to get out of here alive and kicking," said Denver. He sat down.

"Lie down," Caine told them. "Do not speak. Still the heart so the body asks the least air to endure . . . and *hope!*"

Gil said, "You saved me once before. I trust you." He stretched out full-length on the mine floor.

Several of the other men lay down, too. One of them extinguished the other two lanterns.

"I can't simply do nothing," complained Rupp.

But finally he, too, sat down to wait.

TWENTY-SEVEN

Belle had risen quietly out of her bed, dressed
quickly and walked downstairs to the lobby of the
deserted Silver Creek Hotel. The thin blue of dawn
was giving way to the yellow glare of morning out
beyond the tumbledown doors. "Didn't you sleep at
all?"

Boetticher was sitting on a straight-back chair in
the center of the ruined lobby. One booted foot
rested on a squat overturned barrel. "I had an oc-
casional nap."

"Anybody come by to try and make trouble?" she
asked. "I didn't hear anything during the night."

"MacTell, the colored fellow you may have
noticed in the saloon last evening, dropped in around

midnight." Boetticher stood, careful that his spurs didn't become entangled in the tatters of rug around his chair. "We swapped lies about our past lives and accomplishments. I declined to enter into a game of cards. That was pretty much the high point of the evening. Oh, and Estling looked in at an early hour."

"What'd he have to say?"

"Didn't say anything. Merely put his pudgy face up to one of the remains of a window to take a look for himself."

Belle locked her hands behind her back. "Speaking of lies. Do you really have business up at the Lazy Susan Mine?"

"That I do, Miss Belle."

"You're not saying that so you'll have an excuse to look after us?"

"Nope. Like Miss Warden, I'm looking for someone. I have good reason to believe that person will be at the mine."

"Doing a sentence like Gil Conselman?"

"Running the place."

She watched him for a few seconds, her head held a little to the right. "It's not an old friend, though. Not an old friend you're hoping to meet."

"Not exactly, no."

"Jenny's come a long way to find this boy," Belle told him. "Whether that's right or wrong I don't know. But I think she ought to have a chance to find him, talk to him, and . . ."

"What I have to do at the Lucky Susan won't interfere with her plans," said Boetticher. "But what I have to do . . . nothing you can say is going to stop me from doing."

"Can you and Mr. Boetticher continue your conversation in the buckboard?" asked Jenny as she came down the stairs. "I'm ready to leave if you are."

"Allow me to gather your luggage, Miss Warden," said Boetticher, "and we'll be on our way. We don't even have to worry about settling our bill."

"Thank you," she said. She walked across the lobby of the defunct hotel, avoiding the puddles of dirty water, the small mounds of fallen plaster, the piles of mixed debris. "I'll wait out in the wagon."

Boetticher grinned, tipping his hat at her retreating back.

"I don't expect they're going to be too friendly," observed Belle. She drew on the reins, halting the buckboard a few yards from the stockade-style fence that guarded the Lucky Susan Mine.

"Trespassers will be shot," Jenny read from the sign on the fence.

Boetticher took his horse closer to the gate. "Don't seem to be anybody around to do the shooting. No guards peeping over the wall, nobody around the gate at all."

"They can't have abandoned the mine, can they?" asked Jenny.

Boetticher dismounted. "Not likely," he said over his shoulder. "Estling down in Silver Creek would sure have known about it, since it's his job to help out in dragooning fellows to work in the mine. Fancy that, will you?" Grinning, he reached out and pushed at the high, heavy gate.

The gate swung several feet in.

"Careful, Boetticher," cautioned Belle.

He stood listening at the partially open gate. "Something going on inside," he said back to the two girls. "Well, we might as well let ourselves in." He shoved the gate full open, then led his horse through the gateway. His right hand dangled near his holster.

"Do you think something's wrong, Belle?"

"Giddap," Belle told the horses. "Well, they haven't shot us for trespassing yet."

From up ahead, hidden as yet by the office shack, someone yelled, "Quiet! They're tapping back."

"You're imagining things."

"I was just in there, and you can hear it plain."

"That means they're alive."

"Some of them, anyways."

Jenny jumped from the buckboard while Belle was bringing it to a stop. "What's happened? Is Gil Conselman here?" She ran toward the men circling the tunnel entrance.

The men who were waiting their turn to dig and the guards all stood watching the tunnel. No one paid attention to the girl.

Then a slim, dark-haired woman walked over to her. "You've come here looking for Gil Conselman?"

"Yes, but I don't see him . . . is he . . . ?"

Susan nodded. "I'm afraid so. There was a cave-in," she said. "Is he your husband?"

"Not yet."

Susan looked away from the girl and saw the lean dark-clad figure who was walking toward them. "Hello, Rob," she said.

Boetticher didn't slow; the grin didn't leave his face. "Hello, Marianne."

"They call me Susan now."

"Lucky Susan," Boetticher said. He stopped near her.

The midday sun wiped all the shadows from their faces and colored them a stark, glaring gold.

Boetticher said, "So what I heard is true."

"Nobody had to make me come along."

"Where is he? Banner, they call him now."

"Inside the mine."

"He got caught in the cave-in?"

"Yes."

Boetticher watched the dirt being brought out of the tunnel. "How long they figure it's going to take to dig the men out?"

"Until tomorrow morning, probably."

"I can wait that long," said Boetticher. "After all these months, that'll seem like hardly no time at all."

"And what about me?" she asked. "You going to do something to me?"

"You already done it." He walked away toward the tunnel.

TWENTY-EIGHT

The silence in the darkened mine had lasted, Caine feared, about as long as it was going to. He knew from the breathing that no one had managed to go to sleep, and he felt the tension beginning to rise —a pity, he reflected briefly, that meditation was so little practiced in this country. Then, stilling his own thoughts, he sat listening to the messages of the earth's quiet heart.

Across the room Rupp stirred irritably, sat up, and ran his fingers through his yellow hair. "I'm going crazy just waiting. What time is it, anyway?"

A sigh ran through the group, and a rustle of movement.

"About ten minutes past noon." Denver had borrowed Banner's gold watch and was holding it in his left hand.

"Go on, it's got to be later than that."

"Time goes slow when you're doing nothing but waiting in the dark," said Derby.

"That's right," said Rupp. "You know all about the mines, don't you? How come you don't know how to get us out of this one?" He jabbed a finger in the direction of the gold watch. "Sure that thing's running straight? Maybe it got bunged up as bad as Banner."

"It's ticking right along."

"I know we been sitting here more than three hours," insisted the yellow-haired foreman.

"All your gabbing," said Derby, "and all your huffing and puffing ain't doing nothing but burn up air, Rupp."

Rupp, snorting, slumped back against the tunnel wall. His head rolled slowly from left to right and back again, scanning the shadowy ceiling. "We got no guarantee this tunnel ain't going to fall in on us, too. That'd be great, cooling our heels here and waiting to get buried."

"I'd like to see you buried right about now," said old Derby. "To keep you quiet."

Snarling, Rupp lunged at the old man. "I'll save us some air right now, you old cretin."

"Enough!" Caine was suddenly between them. His fingers locked around Rupp's wrist. "If you begin, he will fight back. The struggle to kill him will cost more air than you would save."

"Okay, okay. Let loose of me. I won't kill the old

coot. But you better tell him to stop digging his spurs into me."

When Rupp was again sitting quietly, Caine returned to sit at the side of Banner.

The big man was rolling, feebly, from side to side as he lay on the tunnel floor. He groaned, clutching at himself. In the light from the single lantern his sweat-covered face glowed a flushed red. "I ain't," he said "ain't . . . going to make it."

Caine put his hand on the man's shoulder. "There is yet reason to hope."

"No . . . no hope for Gunther. Gunther's dead and done for." He opened his eyes, watching Caine's face. "That's who . . . who I am. Joshua Gunther. Banner . . . it's only a name I picked for myself . . . got a nice sound to it, you know."

"It does, yes."

"But . . . I'm still the same old Gunther . . . trying to kill you like I did . . . like I killed Dan Boetticher . . . back then . . . I can't . . ."

"Hey," said Rupp, "what's he talking about?"

Caine turned his head toward the foreman. "He does not know what he is saying. Sit quietly, pay no attention."

"Didn't . . . didn't go right this time," said Banner. "No luck lately . . . no luck at all. Only meant to bury you . . . just you, Caine . . . sorry about Gil . . . look better if he goes, too . . . just an accident."

Rupp stood up. "Listen, Banner! Are you responsible for all of us being buried down here?"

Banner's eyes were closed again. He rocked more violently, despite Caine's hand on his shoulder. "Only meant to . . . only the little tunnel . . . must of . . . must of been some kind of fault . . . I didn't know whole thing would·. . ."

Caine was up in time to meet the rushing Rupp. "You will not touch him."

"Like hell. It's because of him we're going to die here," shouted Rupp. "I don't care if he's out of his head or not. I understand good what he's talking about. He tried to rig up some kind of accident for you, and it backfired and caught him and all of us. Give me his gun."

His hand darted toward the wounded man's holster.

Caine anticipated, stepped forward, and caught the foreman's hand in his palm. He spun Rupp around and sent him staggering back to where he had been. "A shot might start another cave-in," he told him as Rupp fell over into a sitting position.

Rupp stayed seated, muttering.

"You should of . . . let him," said Banner, his voice farther away than ever. "It don't make any difference . . ."

"He deserves to die!" Rupp said angrily. "We can do it without the gun. It'd give us *some* time . . ."

"And who will be the next?" Caine demanded, looking from one to another in the dim light. "Will you kill another, and then another, and then another, until you have done to yourselves what the explosion did not?"

Caine did not return to the injured man. Instead, a frown on his lean face, he walked along the tunnel, through the seated men, and toward the blocked exit.

"What is it?" Gil called after him.

Caine stopped and dropped to his knees. He then stretched out, putting his ear to one of the rails of the cart track. "Listen."

The others scrambled to get an ear against metal.

"Tapping," said Denver. "Somebody's tapping on the rails." He grabbed his pick and began clacking the handle on the rail.

Others of the men did the same thing.

"Hold off, now," said Denver. "Give them a chance to come back."

They all listened again, breath held.

"Yep," said Derby. "There it comes again. Three taps and then a pause and then two and then one tap. They're out there sure enough."

Denver sat up, resting his palms on his knees. "Them tracks don't start till the first angle in the tunnel. That means they've come more than ten feet already."

"That's great," sneered Rupp. "They only got about fifty feet more to dig through."

"They're making pretty good time," said Derby.

"Sure," agreed Denver. "There's a good chance they can reach us before the air gives out."

"I think I'll wait a spell before I start celebrating," said Rupp.

TWENTY-NINE

Gil pressed his fingers to the hollow of his throat again, his eyes on the roof of the tunnel. He blinked, shaking his head. "Huh," he said. "For a minute there I had the notion the ceiling was coming down. Not fast like it did off in the side tunnel, but slow. You know, just an inch or so at a time."

Caine gave him an understanding look, but did not speak.

The man was breathing in and out through his mouth, short, choppy breaths. "One thing I ain't imagining. We're running out of air."

Down the line Rupp, who was sprawled against the wall with arms slack at his side, asked, "What time it is now, Denver?"

"Fifteen minutes later than it was last time you asked," replied Denver. "A minute short of being midnight."

"Nowheres near enough air." Rupp clawed a hand down his chest, opening the rest of the buttons of his shirt. "We're not going to make it through to morning."

"We only got five hours to go. Let's all just take it easy, see what happens."

"Geez." A dry rattling sigh came out over Rupp's cracked lips. "I feel like I'm waiting to be taken out to the scaffold."

"Why don't you do like Derby?" suggested Denver. "Go to sleep. By the time you wake up, they may be breaking through."

"Maybe I won't wake up. Maybe I'll open my eyes and be staring smack at the pearly gates."

"Wherever you wake up, Rupp, it ain't going to be anywheres near heaven."

Trying to take in a deeper breath, Gil said to Caine, "You been to different places in the world, places I ain't never even heard of. You done a lot more serious thinking . . . If I die down here, is that it? Do you . . . do you think there's something afterwards, or does it just end?"

"We are all part of the universe," Caine answered, "and that relationship will always continue. But, from time to time, it will change. Death is such a change."

Gil concentrated on his breathing for a moment. "I don't know if I quite understand that."

"It takes a whole lifetime to understand."

"I guess, you know, what's really bothering me is . . . well, I seem to be getting hold of myself again.

I been, since I come to know you, really looking forward to the day I'd finish my sentence here and go back outside. Now it looks sort of like . . . like my life's all over and done."

"We are still a long way from morning," Caine told him. "Many things can happen before then."

"I don't know." Gil rubbed at his throat. "You believe we're going to make it, Caine?"

"Yes."

"You seem awful sure."

"It is only a feeling I have."

"Well, I guess you ain't hardly ever wrong."

Caine smiled. "No, I am wrong as often as any other man. But I try not to let my imagination make my decisions for me."

"I hope we do get out," said Gil. "First thing I'm going to do is write to Jenny again. I been meaning to and meaning to . . . but I haven't for a long time."

"Jenny," said Caine, "she is the girl you love?"

Gil hesitated. "Yes," he said at last. "I guess I do love her. Kind of tough for me to come right out and say it to her, though."

"When we leave here," asked Caine, "you will be able to?"

"Yeah, I will." He let his head sink back against the rock wall. He took short, panting breaths, glancing at the stretched-out Banner. "He seems to be resting a lot easier."

"He is dead," said Caine.

"What?"

"He died a few minutes ago. There was nothing that could be done."

"How come you didn't say anything?"

151

"It is important that we all remain quiet and relaxed," answered Caine. "The others . . . they may think it is an omen."

Gil stared at the body. "The first of us to go," he said.

THIRTY

Earlier that day, at twilight, Susan had walked slowly across the plateau to the house.

She found her husband inside, sitting in the parlor, shoulders hunched, a mug of coffee held in both hands. "You should be out there," she said to him.

"It's no use," said Sterne. "We're never going to dig through in time."

"The men think so."

"They don't know any better." He gulped down coffee. "Anyway, it doesn't much matter now what happens. This finishes the Lucky Susan. God knows what damage's been done down in there. I can't come up with any more money, got no place left to borrow any . . . who are those women?"

"Just now getting curious, Jonathan?"

"You ought to know I've had other things on my mind," he said. "All the guards working to clear the tunnel . . . anybody can walk right in here. And now they know what's going on here, probably, how we been recruiting workers. If they was men, it wouldn't be no problem. We could take care of them one way or other. There was a fellow with them. Who's he?"

"His name is Rob Boetticher."

Sterne stared at her. "Boetticher . . . that was your husband. Is this . . . ?"

"His brother," the dark-haired woman said.

Sterne got up and walked to the window. He couldn't see the mine, but he looked out anyway. "What's he want here, what'd he come for?"

"To kill Banner."

The strength went out of Sterne's hands. The cup fell. "We got to do something. I'll get some of the . . . wait a minute, Susan. Don't he want to kill you, too?"

She watched the coffee stain spreading across the carpet. "Rob was twenty when I married his brother. He's ten years older now, but I imagine he's been thinking of me like I was when Dan first brought me home."

"You're still a handsome woman."

She laughed. "When he saw me today . . . it must have all come to him at once. He realized Banner didn't carry me off against my will, that I had something to do with everything. And that what he'd thought I was a long time ago I'm not any more."

"But if he knows all that, I don't see why . . ."

"Because to him I'm already dead."

Sterne shook his head. "I'll have a couple of the guards—"

"Leave him be. It's between him and Banner now, if Banner ever comes out."

Sterne noticed the coffee cup lying at his feet. He picked it up. "Maybe so," he said. "I guess I've lost my stomach for killing . . . Listen, Susan, I been thinking. I been thinking I want to get away from here. Everything's broke down into too many pieces. I can't put it all together again . . . not even with Banner to help. Let's get away from here, let's leave now."

"That'll be good for you, Jonathan."

"You won't come along?"

"No."

"What do you figure to do?"

"I haven't any idea," she answered.

Nolan took a final bite of the fried chicken leg before flinging it away into darkness. "Something interesting," he said to the bearded guard who was standing at the mouth of the tunnel.

"We're making pretty good progress," he said. "By midnight . . . what'd you say?"

"Just getting around to saying it. I seen Sterne hightailing it out of here."

"Huh?"

"He was in the supply wagon," continued Nolan. "Had it loaded with some of his suitcases and belongings from what I could make out."

"Could be he's only going down to Silver Creek

for help or something. We're going to need a doctor up here and . . ."

"He stopped in the mine office before he took off. I happened to look in there," said Nolan. "That little safe of his is wide open and mighty empty."

"He took what cash there was, even the money that was going to pay our wages?"

"That's what he done."

The guard tugged at his beard. "Seems to me there ain't sense to us working further here, then."

"Yeah, because from now on, we're going to be working for nothing."

"What about Mrs. Sterne?"

"She wasn't with him. Don't know where she's got to."

"Think we got a chance to catch up with Sterne?"

"If he's going to Silver Creek, we should be able to catch him."

The bearded guard headed into the tunnel. "Better tell the rest of the boys. No use their breaking their butts for nothing, either."

Nolan went after him, dodging the workmen who were trundling out earth and rock in barrows.

"Hold on a minute," shouted the bearded guard when he'd reached the site of the digging

Gradually the men halted, turning to look at him. "What is it?" one asked.

The lantern light made the bearded guard seem to grow and shrink. "Thought you all would like to know Mr. Sterne has cleared out."

"What do you mean?" asked a fellow guard.

"He's long gone like a turkey through the corn," explained Nolan. "Took what cash there was left with him. Looks like the Jonathan Sterne Mining Company ain't no more."

"What am I working my tail off for, then?"

"Wait, now," put in a wide workman. "We got a reason to keep working. It don't have nothing to do with Sterne."

"That's right," said Frisco. "We got to get those boys out of there."

"Ain't no use, anyway," said Nolan. "They don't have enough air to last till you reach them."

"We don't know that."

"Suppose," asked Frisco, "it was you in there?"

Nolan shrugged. "It ain't." He gestured at the bearded guard. "Let's get to packing."

"Gentlemen," said Boetticher. He had been working alongside the others, stripped to the waist. The grin was on his face. "I'd advise you not to leave us."

"Who asked you?" said Nolan. "Who are—?"

"Anybody who leaves," Boetticher went on, "is going to be a deserter. And there ain't but one thing to do with deserters."

"Listen, you!" Nolan's hand went to his holster.

But Boetticher's black revolver was already out and aimed. "Forget about it," he advised.

Frisco said, "We ain't got no time to squabble. We got to get to work."

"That's right," said the workman. He resumed digging.

The other workmen followed suit.

None of the guards went back to work.

"Gentlemen," said Boetticher, "you best join in."

"We don't work for you," said the bearded guard.

"Until those men are free, you do." He nodded at Nolan. "About time for you to take a turn with one of the barrows." To the bearded man he said, "And you fill in on a shovel, right over there."

After a brief hesitation they complied.

Susan looked up toward the buckboard. "It's going to get awful cold out here," she told Belle. "You two better come on into the house."

Jenny shook her head. "I want to be here, to watch." She'd taken a light blanket out of her suitcase and had it around her slim shoulders.

"Nothing's going to happen before dawn," said Susan.

"She's right, Jenny. And when Gil does get out, it won't do no good if you're frozen stiff." She got herself to the ground and held out her hand to the auburn-haired girl.

Jenny hesitated. "I couldn't sleep."

"You don't have to sleep," Belle said. "But you need to keep warm."

"I suppose that would be all right." When she was on the ground and they were walking through the chill darkness to the house, she said, "You knew him before, didn't you . . . Mr. Boetticher, I mean."

"Yes, I knew him. A great long while ago."

"But it wasn't you he came here to see."

"No, he wasn't expecting to see me here," said Susan. "Or if he did, he wasn't admitting it to himself."

"I don't really think I like him," said Jenny. "And yet . . ."

158

"You met him too late."

"He was different before?"

"We all were." Susan climbed the steps of the dark house.

The girls followed.

THIRTY-ONE

Gil was lying down now, flat on his back. He breathed shallowly, his lips pulled back from his teeth. His face was a bluish white. "Caine," he gasped out.

"Yes, my friend." Caine sat nearby.

All the others were sprawled out along the tunnel, some asleep, some awake and struggling to breathe. Old Derby kept coughing. Denver was asleep, the gold watch in his open palm; its ticking sounded insistently loud in the stillness. The lantern was sputtering.

"It's late, ain't it?" said Gil.

"About three in the morning."

"I don't want to die," said Gil. "I'm afraid of it."

"Think then of living."

"It's the end."

"Perhaps as waking is the end of sleep," Caine suggested gently.

"No use . . ." The young man passed out.

Caine watched him for a moment, then turned his head to look at the lantern. It was running out of fuel and should be replenished from one of the other lanterns. "I must do that," he told himself.

Instead, his head tipped forward onto his chest.

"Can't be more than eight or ten feet to go," said Frisco as he paused to wipe his face with a ragged orange bandana.

"We got to run them some air in there," said the wide workman. "So as to make sure they last till we get through to them."

"Already thought of that." Two other workers were approaching with a ten-foot length of two-inch pipe. "We can drive this through that rubble and it'll take in air from out here," continued the one at the head end of the pipe. He fitted a metal cap over the pipe end. "Keep it from filling up with junk whilst it's traveling through."

The wide man nodded his head, smiling. "That ought to do it." He rubbed his big hands together and took up a sledge hammer. "Set her in place."

The other two climbed the pile of rubble with the pipe and rammed it into the earth.

The wide miner swung the hammer.

"Not budging," said one of the others.

Another blow struck the free end of the pipe, and another.

"She's moving," said Frisco.

The wide man kept at it, swinging the heavy sledge again and again. Finally, his face glistening with a fresh sweat, he said, "That's it, feels like she's through."

The front man on the pipe had dropped to the ground. "Got a twelve-foot rod back here. I'll fetch her."

After the rod was inserted into the pipe, the wide man lifted the hammer again. "There," he said, after two swings. "Cap's popped off free." He shoved the rod a good foot forward to make sure before fingering it rapidly out.

"They got air now," said Frisco. "Everything's going to be okay."

Licking his lips, the wide man put his mouth to the free end of the pipe. "Hey, in there!" he shouted. "Hey, in there. Can you hear me?"

He got his ear close to the pipe.

After a full minute Frisco asked, "They answering?"

"No," said the wide man.

Caine dreamed he was in the air, out beyond the edge of a precipice. Yet he did not fall. He hung suspended high above jagged rocks and a rushing stream.

Suddenly his head hit the ground. He was awake, realizing he'd tipped over sideways while he slept. He braced his hands on the gritty tunnel floor in order to push himself up. "I am like one new-born," he reflected when he found he hadn't the strength to rise.

He heard something then. The sound of rocks falling. Not falling from above, but from somewhere down the tunnel. Rocks trickling down an incline.

Caine strained to hear. There was only silence now.

After a moment there came a metallic sound.

"Someone breaking through to us," he thought. He began, slowly and deliberately, to pull himself along the ground.

It seemed to take him a great deal of time. Finally he was able to get up to his hands and knees and move along that way.

He heard a new sound, a faint rasping. Then something that might be a voice calling, from a long way off.

Caine kept crawling.

He saw the end of the pipe protruding from the rubble and could feel already that air, fresh air, was coming in from outside.

"We're close now!" said a voice through the pipe. "Can you hear me?"

He worked his way to the pipe end and pulled himself up close to it. He meant to say, "I hear you," but his voice came out only as a dry croak.

Picking up a rock, he began to tap on the metal.

"Is that you?" asked the outside voice. "Do you hear us?"

Caine tapped again.

After a moment he made another attempt to speak. "We . . . are . . . alive," he was able to say.

Then he lay back against the rocks and began to take deep breaths.

THIRTY-TWO

Caine shook Gil gently by the arm. "Wake up, my friend," he said. "We will soon be free."

The blond young man sat up. He took a breath, a deep one, and that surprised him. "Air!" he said, laughing. "There's air coming in again."

"They were able to get a pipe through from outside a few moments ago."

Down the line, old Derby sat up suddenly, coughing violently. "I'm still alive," he announced, chuckling. "And I can smell air, even over the scents of all you unwashed galoots."

Denver was awake, holding the gold watch to his ear before again checking the time. "A shade after five," he said. "We made it through to morning."

Derby went tottering along the tunnel toward the air pipe. "That's because they rammed a tube through," he said. "Right smart, especial for fellows who ain't had much experience in the mines."

"Well, Rupp, things ain't as bad as they was when you dozed off," Denver told the slow-rising foreman.

Rubbing one hand across his tangled yellow hair while he wiped crusting out of his eyes with the other, Rupp said, "Don't kid yourself it was anything to do with any feelings they have about us. It's plain and simple a business proposition. Sterne needs us to keep working his mine."

"Whether they did it for love or money," said Denver, "it feels good to be alive and still breathing."

Rupp took a big lung-filling breath, then sauntered over to Caine. "Now that we got plenty of air, Mr. Chinaman, would it be all right with you if we did a little digging from our side? So as to meet them boys out there halfway."

"Do as you wish," said Caine.

Gil made an angry noise. "Nothing's ever going to change you, is it, Rupp? Why, you know dang well if it wasn't for following Caine's advice and listening to what he told us to do, we'd all be dead now."

"You want to go around thinking you owe your life to some sad-faced Chinaman," said Rupp, "you go right ahead." He tapped his own chest with grimy fingers. "It's 'cause of me, nobody else, that I'm alive."

"A real shame, too," said Gil.

Rupp walked over to the body of Banner. "How come you ain't sitting up and taking credit for saving us, Mr. Banner? Everybody else is, and . . . He's dead! Stiff as a board."

"What's that?" asked Denver.

Caine told him, "Mr. Banner died last night. His injuries were very serious. Even had we been rescued much earlier, he would probably not have lived."

"No skin off my nose," said Rupp as he turned away. "Got caught in his own trap."

Denver stroked a finger along his nose. "This is going to change things outside," he said. "It's always looked to me like Banner there was the backbone of this whole operation."

"Sterne's not going to be so tough now," said Gil.

"We can kick all this around later." Rupp located his pick and went striding toward the blocking rubble. "Now it's time for some serious digging. Come on, the rest of you."

Gil held back, staying at Caine's side. "You think maybe we could win in a showdown with Sterne and the guards?"

"That may not be necessary."

"But even if we get out," Gil said, "wouldn't we still be wanted by the law?"

"Mr. Banner was a law unto himself. He and Mr. Sterne have done things for which there is no legal justification," said Caine. "Once we are clear of the gates of the Lucky Susan Mine I do not think we will be pursued either by Mr. Sterne or by anyone else."

"Well, that sounds pretty good," said Gil. "Then maybe in a few days I'll really be free. I can write to Jenny or . . ." He didn't let himself finish the sentence.

"Or? What is it you wish, my friend?"

"Well, I been thinking about maybe going back home, for a while," said Gil. "You know, so I could actually see Jenny. I'd have to work a spell first to get fare money, but . . . the only thing is, I don't know if I can face her or the rest of them back there."

"You have faced much worse things," reminded Caine. "You have even faced death. From now on, lesser encounters should not trouble you."

Gil smiled. "That's right," he said.

THIRTY-THREE

"We done broke through," yelled Frisco.

In another few minutes there was a large enough opening for men to pass through.

The wide man went in first. "Some of them we're going to maybe have to carry out."

Boetticher pushed his way through the cluster of workmen. He went through the hole second.

Inside, three lanterns were burning. Most of the trapped men were crowded near the new opening.

"No need for you to come tromping all over everybody," Rupp was saying to the wide man. "Just move your fat carcass out of the way so we can start getting clear of here."

"I thought you might . . . oh, what the hell, Rupp.

168

I should of known better than to expect as much as a thank-you out of you."

"We appreciate what you done," said Denver, holding out his hand. "Thanks a real lot."

"You're welcome." The wide man took the hand and shook it. "It's good to see you all again, most of you, anyhow."

Rupp gave him a shove, headed for the way out.

Boetticher asked Derby, "Whereabouts is Banner?"

"Back yonder."

Boetticher walked slowly down the tunnel. He saw a tall figure bending. "Banner?" he called softly, his hand near his holster.

Caine straightened to face him. "Mr. Banner is dead," he said.

"What?" Boetticher took three more steps.

"He was injured when the cave-in occurred," explained Caine. "He was a friend of yours?"

The grin returned briefly to Boetticher's face. "No."

Caine studied him. "Yet you have come a long way to find him."

Easing closer, Boetticher stood looking down at the dead man. "He killed my brother."

Nodding, Caine said, "Then you are Mr. Boetticher."

"How'd you know that?"

"Before he died, Mr. Banner spoke of a man he had killed."

"Deathbed confession, huh?"

"He felt the need to talk," said Caine. "It is very difficult for some men to die alone."

"We all got to die that way."

"Mr. Banner had not realized that," said Caine. "And what will you do now?"

Boetticher lifted his eyes from the dead man. "I don't rightly know," he said. "Only purpose my life's had for a long time now has been to find the three men who murdered my brother."

"You have found the other two?"

"Yeah, them I found alive."

"You left them dead?"

Boetticher said, "That's what I promised myself I'd do."

"Now destiny has robbed you of Mr. Banner," said Caine, "and the purpose has been taken from your existence."

Boetticher asked, "Who are you, anyway?"

"My name is Caine." He bent again and, without seeming to strain, lifted the body of the dead man. "I must take him out of here."

Boetticher didn't say anything for a time. He watched Caine carrying Banner away.

When Caine was a few yards away, he turned and said, "I hope, Mr. Boetticher, you will be able to find some new reason for living."

Gil had taken two dozen steps into the bright clear morning when he saw her. She was standing at the edge of the crowd, one slender hand touching her cheek, straining to see each man as he emerged. "Jenny," he said, and louder again, "Jenny!"

"Gil!"

They ran to each other, meeting on a patch of

rocky ground, surrounded by dirt-smeared workmen.

"You're here," he said to her after a while.

"Yes, I decided I'd better come and . . . is that all right, Gil?"

"It's all right, yes. It's fine, Jenny." He let go of her, standing back. "Listen, I may have to serve a little more time here. We're going to have to have a showdown with Sterne, but then . . ."

"Sterne is gone," said the girl. "I heard them talking about it. And as soon as they dug through to you . . . the guards, most of them, took off as well."

"You mean Sterne's gone for good?"

"As I understand it."

"Then the whole thing here has fallen apart," laughed Gil. "I'm free right this minute. Hey, that's simply fine."

Jenny said, "You said 'but then' a minute ago, Gil. What was that going to lead to?"

"Oh, I was going to invite you to get married."

"I'd like that, yes."

Gil nodded to himself. "Yeah, that was easy."

They moved off together, away from the others, talking. The men were hurrying off to the bunkhouses, elated at their freedom, eager only to gather up what possessions they had and leave the Lucky Susan forever.

Caine began digging a grave with a shovel and the pick he had used for digging silver. When he had buried Banner, he too would leave—but for where? The curious sense of a new course, a changing wind, he had had when Banner was bringing him to the mine had been false, it seemed. The mine had brought him to no one who knew of Daniel Caine.

His pick rang dully on the rocky soil as he worked. Because he had chosen a spot near the mine entrance, he was not wholly surprised when he uncovered a vein of ore, but neither was he pleased. What use had Banner for silver now?

"Caine! Hey, Caine!" It was Gil, running toward him, holding the woman Jenny by the hand. Both looked supremely happy.

"Caine, guess what!" Gil demanded. "Jenny knows your brother!"

Somewhat breathlessly, Jenny explained, "At least, he was named Daniel Caine. In Virginia City, where we had a four-day stand. He was staying at the same hotel our troupe was at, and he—we used to talk sometimes. He might still be there. I hope it's the right person. Mr. Caine, I understand you saved Gil's life. And 'thank you' isn't strong enough, but— we do thank you," she ended shyly.

"He saved his own life," Caine said. "Thank you for telling me about this Daniel Caine. I will go there, after I have finished."

They looked down silently at the half-dug grave, and to the blanket-covered form beyond. Then, with a flurry of goodbyes, the two were gone, and Caine went back to his digging.

No one came to the burial.

Except Boetticher. He stood by, watching. When Caine had filled the grave with earth he said, "I'll be moving on."

Caine patted the earth down with the flat of the shovel. He did not speak.

"She was here, too," went on Boetticher. "My brother's wife. I thought they'd carried her off after they killed him, but that wasn't how it was, at all. She went along of her own free will. From what I heard around here, she wasn't Banner's woman no more. She'd gone over to this fellow Sterne." His eyes narrowed as he looked up at the bright late-morning sky. "No sign of her around here. She must have rode off by herself during the night."

Caine walked down the slight incline toward the toolshed to return the shovel he'd used to dig Banner's grave. After he'd done that, he said to Boetticher, "Have you decided what you will do now?"

"Nope." Boetticher shrugged. "Any suggestions?"

"Live," Caine told him.

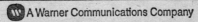